CAMBRIA HEBERT

CAMBRIA HEBERT

Jingle Bells
Christmas smells
Chopping down a tree
Travis states: Santa's fake!
Oh for goodness sake!

Trent, Drew, and the entire hashtag crew are back for holiday shenanigans! When Travis declares, "Santa's fake!" the family bands together to deliver Christmas magic and the joy of family into the heart of a little boy who never had a reason to believe.
What ensues will make you laugh, cry, and perhaps remind you what it's like to see the holidays through the eyes of a child.
So what's it going to be: Christmas chaos or happily ever after?
Maybe a little bit of both.

In addition to a **brand new** holiday-themed short story, this special edition of *GearShark* includes a holiday-themed interview with Trent and Drew, nine scrumptious recipes, *The Prank*—a holiday bonus scene featuring Trent and Drew—and fun Christmas trivia to test your holiday knowledge!

#HEA is a short story but is book seven in the *GearShark* series. This is not a standalone.

*"May you never be too grown up to search the skies on
Christmas Eve."*
—author unknown

Happy Holidays!
Cambria Hebert

THE PRANK

A HOLIDAY BONUS SCENE
FEATURING TRENT AND DREW

*This scene is placed first in this book because it takes place
BEFORE Trent and Drew are married, before Drew's
accident, and before they become dads.
This was written in 2018, but this is the first time it is in print.*

Trent

"Tell me again why we're doing this," I prompted as we stomped through the fallen leaves and a bitter wind brushed over my cheeks.

"It's tradition," Drew grumped from behind.

I couldn't help but smile. Dude made me come out here every year to cut down a damn tree for our living room, demanding that it was absolutely necessary. But while we were doing it, he acted like a racoon with a butt rash.

On impulse, I spun around and stopped abruptly. Drew wasn't paying attention and collided right into me.

Automatically, my arms came out to steady him. "Whoa."

"What the hell?" he muttered, but then our eyes met.

I loved that we were about the same height and whenever we stood like this, our eyes were on the same level. It made it easy to look into him.

"Hi."

A small smiled played at the corners of his mouth. "Why'd you stop walking?"

"Just wondering why you insist on this tradition every year when it makes you cranky as hell."

"I'm not cranky," he rebuked.

I grinned.

He made a sound. "It's just balls cold out here is all." His eyes shifted away, and a I knew he was lying.

But why?

"Your cheeks are red," I told him, rubbing my gloved hands together and then cupping his face to offer some warmth.

His blue eyes came back to mine, and warmth sparked inside. "So are yours."

I made a sound. "Don't worry about me, Forrester. I'm good as long as you are."

Drew leaned in and kissed me. My fingers tightened on his face, and I held him close. His arms went around my waist, and we kissed in the middle of the woods while the wind blew around us.

Eventually, he drew back, but I still held his face, rubbing my thumbs over his cheeks.

Reaching up between us, he tugged the beanie I was wearing down over my ears a little farther. "You're going to get sick."

I stepped back, reaching for his hand. "How about we just go to the mall and get a tree there like most of America?"

"Hells no." Drew denied and tugged me deeper into the woods.

I went along with him because, honestly, I'd go anywhere Drew went. And clearly, cutting down our own tree was something that was important to him. I guess I would just have to resign myself to doing this for the rest of my life.

A little while later, I saw a tree and pointed it out. "How about that one?"

"Too small."

We kept walking.

"That one?" I asked a bit later.

"It's crooked."

I balked. "Crooked?"

Drew made a sound, grabbed my shoulders, and moved me until I was in the correct position to see how "crooked" the tree was. With his chest against my back, he reached around me and pointed. "See?"

"How am I supposed to see anything when you're pressed up against me?"

Drew grabbed my hand and spun me around. "Pervert."

I smiled. "You made me that way."

"Come on, then." He tugged me along, and we kept searching.

"This one!" Drew finally declared twelve hundred years later.

I turned toward the one he was pointing to. "It looks like the first one I picked out."

"This one is bigger."

I smirked. "Size matters, does it?"

"You made me that way," he quipped, echoing what I'd told him earlier.

"All right," I said, feeling pretty proud of myself. "Let's have the saw. I'll cut it down."

"I'll do it," he said, brandishing the tool.

I watched him basically crawl beneath the lower branches, firing a few low curse words as he went. Stifling a laugh, I went behind him to enjoy the view of his fine ass sticking out from under the branches.

"Are you staring at my ass?" he called out a few moments later.

"Of course I am."

The sound of a saw working its way through the tree trunk filled the woods, and I gazed around our property, appreciating the fact that we had so many acres and the ability to cut down a tree like this in privacy.

Romeo had a damn fine idea to buy all this land and build our family a compound.

"Almost there," Drew called out, his voice muffled from all the branches.

With a wicked thought, I moved around to the other side, watching the tree wobble and tilt as it was about to fall over.

"Timber!" he yelled like a professional lumberjack.

Dude was really getting into this crap.

When the tree was about to fall, I went with my impish idea. Catching the large tree wasn't really a problem, so I did but then fell onto the ground with it, making sure it covered me.

"Ahhh!" I yelled as though I were crushed. "Shit, it hit me!"

The tree Drew insisted upon was definitely big, and it pretty much covered my entire body. It was actually kinda heavy.

"Trent!" Drew yelled, and I heard him scrambling around nearby. "Shit! Trent!"

"Ow," I called out and made some pathetic sounds.

The sound of cursing drifted between the branches, and his booted feet came into view. "Oh, fuck, T," Drew spat, worry taking over his voice.

The weight of the tree was suddenly gone, tossed aside. One of the branches caught my cheek and scraped as it was ripped away, and I sucked air through my teeth with the sting.

Drew dropped beside me on both knees, his hands hovering over me as I turned my face toward him.

He growled, frustrated. "You're bleeding."

Using his teeth, he ripped off the gloves covered in sap and pine needles, tossing them aside. His warm fingers lay against my cheek and pushed my face closer.

Leaning close, he studied the cut on my cheek and cursed low.

"Trent." He worried. "You okay? Is anything broken?"

I made a sound, and he freaked out all over again.

"This is all my fault! I never should have made you come look for this damned tree. Fuck!" He sat back on his haunches and shoved a hand through his hair.

"You too worked up to give me mouth to mouth?" I asked.

Drew's eyes flew to my face. The worry there shifted, and then his stare narrowed. "Are you fucking with me right now?" he demanded.

A low laugh built in the back of my throat. "No, I really need mouth to mouth."

Drew burst up to his feet and paced. "What the hell, T? God, I thought that tree fell on you and crushed you! I was about to call 9-1-1!"

Okay, so maybe my little prank wasn't so funny after all.

Pushing up off the ground, I stood and reached for him.

He shoved my arm away and stepped back.

"Forrester…" I began, reaching out again.

His chest heaved when he turned to glare. "There is no joke—never will be—that I will find funny if it implies you getting hurt."

Holding up both my hands, palms out, I apologized. "I'm sorry. I didn't think you'd get that upset."

"What would you have done if a nine-foot tree fell on me?"

I cringed. "Point taken."

He cursed again. "You're bleeding."

I used the back of my hand to dab at the blood on my cheek. "It's just a scrape. I'm fine."

He made an impatient sound and came forward as he pulled the sleeve of his hoodie out from under the sleeve of his coat. Gripping my chin with one hand, he used the other to dab the sleeve against the cut.

It stung, but I acted like it was nothing because clearly, I'd already upset him enough.

He was still dabbing at it when I grabbed his wrist and pulled his hand down.

"Hey," I said, soft.

His eyes moved to mine.

"I'm sorry. For real. It was just a joke."

"You getting hurt is not a joke."

"Yeah." I sighed. "You're right."

Cupping his face, I pivoted so I was standing directly in front of him. "Can you forgive me?"

He made an ugly face. "No." He pulled away and reached for the tree, manhandling it into a standing position.

"Drew."

"C'mon. Let's get this back. It's fucking cold."

I stared at him incredulously. "Forrester."

He grunted and tossed the tree back onto the ground, swinging around. "You think I want to be out here doing this shit? I do it for you, goddammit! And what the hell do you do? You take ten years off my life by making me think I crushed you with a tree!"

Okay, whoa.

I blinked, and silence fell between us. A strong gust of wind kicked up, ruffling all the trees around us, surrounding us with the scent of pine and snow. I glanced up at the sky, noting how gray it looked.

It was definitely going to snow tonight.

"You're out here doing this for me?" I asked, low. "I thought you said it was tradition."

"*Our* tradition!" He fumed.

Caught off guard, I drew up short. Blinking, I looked at his face, which was a mixture of hurt and anger.

Shit. I really fucked up this time.

I moved forward, stepping near so there was barely any distance between us. Drew started to move away, but I caught his arm and pulled him back. "Stay put."

He practically snarled at me, but his feet stayed where they were.

"You don't actually like coming out here to cut down a tree, do you?"

"Seriously, T. Who the fuck actually likes doing this?"

"Rimmel," I deadpanned.

Drew snorted. "I should call Romeo to commiserate over beer."

I grabbed his shoulder. "You ain't commiserating. Especially not over anything to do with me."

His eyes lifted to mine, and I pinned the blue irises

with a stare. "You didn't do this when you were growing up?"

Drew made a rude sound. "Hell no. My dad drove us to a tree lot and bought the first one my sister pointed to."

I rocked back a little, my hand slipping off his shoulder. "So this is just something you and I have done?"

He gave me a *no shit* look.

Guilt slammed into me. Guilt for ever complaining about the cold, for all the times I said we should just get a fake tree at the mall. For pulling a prank when clearly the guy was trying to do something meaningful.

"You wanted to do this so we had a tradition of our own," I murmured.

Drew turned away, but I caught his arm.

"Drew."

Turning back, he answered but didn't look at me. "It appalls me that your mother only ever put up a tabletop fake-ass Charlie Brown tree when you were growing up," he answered. "That you grew up in a house where you were mostly alone and holidays weren't anything but a reminder that your mom never made anything special."

It felt as if he'd just punched through my chest and grabbed my heart. It hurt. It physically ached in the center of my ribs, and subconsciously, I reached up and rubbed a palm over my chest.

"I want you to have better. I wanted to give you memories and traditions, shit that made you feel like you're part of a family. Part of something special." Drew scrubbed a hand over his face and sighed. "It's stupid."

The place below my ribcage felt hollow and tender. I didn't have words. I didn't have any way of expressing exactly just how much this confession moved me.

Stirring suddenly, I grabbed him, yanking him close. My arms clamped around him, and I hugged as tight as I could, squishing his big body against mine. Resting my chin on his shoulder, I felt my heart pound erratically, and I squeezed my eyes closed.

After a moment, his arms came around me to hug me back.

I clung to him, shifting even closer, wishing I could crawl inside his skin and live there.

"Trent," he said after a while of me crushing him close.

I pulled back but dove into his mouth, kissing him fiercely, bulldozing his body back until he came up against a large tree. Drew planted his feet wide, and I stepped between his legs, tangling my tongue with his so thoroughly I wouldn't have known which one was mine.

A low rumble vibrated my throat, and I tilted my head the opposite way and continued to kiss him deeply.

Eventually, I had to come up for air. Eventually, I had to pull away in hopes my heart might not burst. Even still, I stayed close, caging his body against the tree.

"I seriously thought there was no way I could love you more." My voice was throaty. "But I just fell even harder."

Drew reached around to shove his hands in the back pockets of my jeans. His palms molded against my ass, and I pressed even closer against him.

"The fact that you are willing to do all this…" I gazed around the woods and half smiled. "That you even have those thoughts…" I cupped his cheek. "Forrester, it erases every unpleasant or lonely memory I might have about Christmas."

"I can't get it outta my head, T. The mini version of you sitting alone at home."

"Don't," I said, leaning in to kiss him softly. "Think of us putting up this monster tree and arguing over who's going to untangle the lights. Think of us getting drunk on spiked eggnog and only getting half the tree decorated tonight because we fall into bed. Think of Christmas morning in bed together, those quiet moments before we go watch all the kids rip into their gifts."

"Is that what you think of?" he asked, his stare penetrating mine.

I nodded. "It is. Every thought centers around you. The holidays are special because I have you."

He glanced away, and I forced his stare back. "And because you do sentimental shit like this."

He scoffed. "That you try and ruin with bad jokes."

I kissed him again. "I'm sorry." Another kiss. "For reals."

Stepping back, I laid a hand over my heart. "From now on, I will be on my best behavior when we are cutting down a Christmas tree."

"Fuck that. Next year, I'm getting one at the mall."

"Hells no!" I declared. "This is our tradition."

Drew's eyes softened. "Neither of us like doing this."

"I like doing it now. It's my favorite thing for Christmas."

He snorted.

"I love you, Forrester."

I knew by the look on his face that he wasn't mad anymore.

With a sound, he dabbed at my cheek some more. "You're bleeding again."

Catching his wrist, I pulled it away from my face and threaded our fingers together. "C'mon. We gotta get this monster home so we can decorate it."

As we carried it through the woods on the way back to our place, Drew glanced over his shoulder at me. "I was thinking of another tradition we could maybe start."

"Lay it on me."

"Sex under the tree."

"Hells yeah!"

Drew's laughter carried with the wind and wrapped around my heart.

It was going to be a very Merry Christmas.

ONE

TRENT

> *Once upon a Christmas season,*
> *All was merry and bright,*
> *Until a little boy made a declaration and caused a big fight...*

"SANTA'S FAKE!"

The words dropped into the family's traditional pancake Sunday like a grenade with no delay. My son's words were punctuated by the sound of his fork clattering against his plate, the clang echoing through the almost shocked silence that immediately followed.

All the adults at the table glanced around, wondering if anyone else heard exactly what he said. Almost as if we prayed to God we'd heard him wrong.

But no.

We all heard the same thing.

Santa's fake.

"Trav," I said, reaching into the stunned silence, looking for even more confirmation I didn't need. "What did you just say?"

"Santa's fake, Dad. So is Christmas."

Across the table, Rimmel's mouth dropped open. Beside me, Drew's hand settled on the top of my thigh as his body stiffened.

"Is not!" Nova burst out. "Santa is too real!"

"Yeah!" Blue echoed. "He comes here every year!"

"Nuh-uh!" Travis argued. "Liar!"

"Whoa," I declared.

"He's not a liar! You're a liar!" Jax yelled.

Travis pushed back from his chair, his face a mask of anger and hurt. "Santa is not real! My mom said so. She said Christmas isn't real either."

My heart squeezed, and my son's declaration rang inside my head so forcefully I wondered briefly if one could suffer a concussion just from words.

Asher started crying, and Rimmel jumped up to console him.

"Look what you did!" Nova insisted, pointing at Asher. "You made him cry!"

Travis glanced at Rimmel and Asher, then around at everyone who was practically stunned. His face fell, and he ran from the room, his feet making light pounding sounds as he went.

Drew stood, cradling Andi in his arms.

"I'll go," I told him, already on the move.

"T." His voice brought me around just as easily as if he had reached out and touched me with his hand.

His eyes asked me many questions, though his lips spoke not one word. *Did you know about this? How could we not know? Our son doesn't believe in Christmas? Who the fuck tells a little boy there is no Santa?*

We knew when we adopted two kids who had been born into no place children ever belonged, it would be a long road. I expected it. Drew expected it. It could be daunting at times, but our son and daughter made it worth it.

This, though?

This, no one expected. Of all the obstacles I knew we would face, having a child who didn't believe in Christmas seemed tragic.

"I'll be back," was all I said, giving apologetic looks to everyone I passed as I left the room.

The front door was still slightly ajar, and one of Rim's dogs, Ralph, was standing with his nose pressed into the crack and his tail wagging.

Crisp fall air swirled inside when I pulled it open, and Ralph rushed out ahead of me. Travis was sitting on the top step, French Fry lying beside him.

The second Ralph lunged down the steps, Fry took off after him, and the two looked like big puppies running around in the leaves coating the driveway.

Travis didn't turn and look. He didn't move from his seated position with his arms tightly wrapped around his indrawn knees.

As I lowered beside him, the brisk wind blew, ruffling my hair and kissing my cheeks. Frowning, I noticed he was only wearing a long-sleeved shirt with his sweat-pants. Unzipping the hoodie I had on, I pulled it around him.

"It's too cold to be out here without a coat." My voice was calm.

His was not. "I don't care!"

"Well, I care." I insisted. "Put your arms in."

He made a sound but did as I asked. My hoodie was twelve times too big, but it looked cute as hell. So cute it hurt. It pained me that such a small boy could be robbed of something so innocent and pure so early in life.

The tip of his nose was already pink and so were the

tops of his ears. The glossy black hair on his head blew in the breeze, so I pulled the hood up to offer a little more protection.

"You want to tell me what happened back there?" I asked, keeping my voice casual.

Farther down the driveway, the dogs barked and ran. Multicolored leaves fell from the trees, swirling in the air before gently landing on the ground.

"I didn't lie!" He insisted, his voice forceful and angry from inside the hood.

Hooking one finger around the edge of the hood, I peeled it back just enough to see his face. "I know you didn't. You aren't in trouble."

We told him that a lot. He often thought he would be punished or scolded for most of the things he did. He'd been getting better now that he'd been with us for about six months, but there were still rough days.

How did you help a child overcome five years of basic neglect and mistreatment? I knew it was possible, but those first five years of his had left their mark... or should I say scar? They would always be there. They would always be part of who he was.

I didn't necessarily want to undo that, because I loved this kid how he was. But I did want him to have the innocence most other kids had. I didn't want him to be hardened and bitter.

His silence was practically mutiny, and I might have smiled because his stubborn strength was something I actually admired, but I couldn't smile. How could I when I knew what taught him such a trait?

"You don't believe in Santa?"

Tucking his arms tightly around his body, he peaked around the hood. "No."

My throat felt thick, words felt foreign, and I wasn't sure I wanted to know the answer, but I didn't have a choice. A good parent never did. A good parent did the hard stuff so the kid didn't have to.

"Your mom told you he wasn't real?"

We didn't talk about his mom much. He rarely mentioned her, so the fact he did now told me this was a big thing for him.

He nodded.

"Have you ever had a Christmas tree?"

He shook his head.

I looked away, focusing across the property, noting the fall-heavy sky and the hint of snow in the air. Even though I tried to focus on those things as I tried to compose myself, I couldn't.

All I could think about was mine and Drew's tradition. How we cut down a giant tree every single year. All I could think about was the reason behind it. How hurt Drew was on my behalf when he realized I'd spent a lot of holidays alone with a tabletop tree and not much else.

I didn't think it was that big of a deal. I mean, I was fine. I understood now.

I understood in a way that made me ache. In a way that made me so incredibly grateful for Drew.

This boy, this brave, strong kid who literally saved his sister's life, had never had a Christmas. He didn't know what it was to have boisterous, loud holidays like we did now.

I wanted so much in that moment to do two things:

1. Grab my son and hug him tight and give him everything he never had.

and

2. Bury my face in Drew's neck, hug him as tight as

his bones would allow, and tell him how much I loved everything he'd given me over the years.

Going to Drew wasn't an option right now because this boy came before me.

Plucking him off the step, I pulled him into my lap. His arms stayed tight around his middle, but he didn't try to escape my hold.

"Santa never came to visit you before, huh?"

"Because I'm not a good boy," he wailed and burst into tears.

My body rocked slightly back under the force with which he threw himself against me. His thin shoulders shook under the extra fabric of my hoodie, and his cries were muffled against my chest.

The pounding of my heart could be heard over the sound of my forced swallows. Folding my arms around him, I covered the back of his head with my entire palm. "Aw, Trav," I rasped. "That's not true, son. You are the best boy I know."

Movement behind us made me turn. Drew stepped out onto the porch, his eyes narrowed as he assessed the situation. I gave him a grim look and then let him see a little flash of anger I harbored deep down for the woman who gave birth to my son.

His lips rolled inward, and the scruff on his jaw shifted as he digested what I hadn't said and then gently settled beside us.

The outside of his thigh was warm against mine.

Over the hood, I rubbed the back of Travis's head, trying to reassure him. "I promise you aren't a bad boy."

Drew's thigh jolted against mine, and our eyes met briefly.

"Then if Santa is real and I'm not a bad boy, how come he never visited me before?"

I felt the change in Drew. I knew he was being pummeled. I wanted to hold his hand, but I couldn't let go of our son. Knowingly, Drew's fingers pushed between my bicep and my body, his arm looping through mine, linking us together.

Strength suffused me, his presence offering me assurance.

"You're a big kid, so I'm going to tell you the truth, okay?"

I felt him nod against my chest.

"I like your mom." I began, realizing the words didn't stick inside my swollen throat as much as I expected. In fact, saying them out loud made me feel a kind of freedom I didn't realize I needed to feel.

Drew looked at me, his nose wrinkling, and I knew he was likely thinking I was insane. It was sort of unspoken between us that Travis's birth mother wasn't our favorite person.

But you know… that wasn't right.

"You know why I like her?"

Travis shook his head again.

"'Cause without her, I would never have you. Without her, we wouldn't have your sister. And because of that, I could never, ever hate her."

"She wasn't very nice." Travis's small voice made my heart crack.

Drew's eyes flared, and angry emotion dashed across his face.

I shook my head slightly, and his lip curled.

"I know, bud. Your mom had a lot of problems, and unfortunately, she didn't have any friends to help her out. So she made a lot of really bad choices, and she didn't take care of you and Andi the way she should have."

Travis lifted his face, dark eyes rising toward mine. "Santa didn't come because Mom was bad?"

Oh, the innocence. I wasn't sure if I should be sadder about the fact that this question proved he still embodied it or that it was a question he had to ask.

I shared a look with Drew, then went back to Travis. "Well, maybe Santa was upset at some of the choices she made. But that doesn't mean she was all bad." I tapped his chest with my finger. "No one who could make you could ever be all bad."

"Santa couldn't find you," Drew announced, sort of like he was coming to the rescue with a much more kid-friendly answer.

"He couldn't?" Travis asked, perking right up and turning toward his dad.

Drew nodded. "How could he when you didn't have a tree? Or lights or reindeer food put out for the reindeer!"

"Reindeer food?" Travis's little pink nose wrinkled. "What's that?"

Drew looked at me. I blinked. I had no idea what the fuck reindeer food was.

He cleared his throat. "Ah, you know. It's the stuff that you sprinkle outside for them to eat. That way when they're flying through the sky, they can smell it and know to stop."

I suppressed a smile. Dude was good at making up shit on the fly.

Travis's eyes turned wide and curious. The second they focused on me, I nearly melted. "You put out reindeer food too?"

"Ah, sure. We put out cookies for Santa too. It's a lot of work delivering toys. Big man gets hungry. He needs a snack."

"I like cookies!"

"We know." Drew nodded.

Kid ate like a trucker. I could only imagine how much he would eat when he was a teenager.

"And we cut down a tree every year. And put up lights and have parties," I told him.

Interest sparked in his eyes, and it was so much better than the flat-out denial I'd seen before.

"You believe in Christmas?"

"Of course!" I scoffed.

Trav looked at Drew, who nodded vehemently. "Me too."

"You believe in Santa?"

"How could I not? I've seen him with my own two eyes," Drew announced, pointing at his peepers.

"You know Santa Claus!" Travis announced, shocked and awed at the same time.

Behind him, I gave Drew a look. Dude was taking it a little too far.

He ignored the look I knew he saw me lasering in his direction and focused solely on our son.

"This one year, I stayed up all night just to catch him in the act."

"Did you see him?"

"'Course." Drew scoffed. "Caught him going right up the chimney and saw the reindeer outside!"

"They must like that reindeer food!"

I wanted to groan.

Drew plucked the boy out of my lap, tucking him into his. Even if I was rather put out by his over-the-top Christmas details, I couldn't be upset. Just seeing him sitting there smiling down at Trav was enough to make my heart flutter.

"Dad, if we make it this year, do you think I can see a reindeer too?"

Drew blanched, and a laugh bubbled up out of me. Dude was in deep.

"I don't see why not."

"Thanks, Dad!" Travis burst out, wrapping his arms around Drew's neck. Over his shoulder, Drew smiled.

"Nova! Blue!" Travis bellowed, scrambling off Drew's lap and rushing toward the front door. "My dad says we're going to see Santa's reindeer!"

"Hey, Tra—"

But Drew's call was wasted on deaf ears. Our son was already halfway through the house, shouting about reindeer and seeing Santa.

A few seconds later, his ocean-blue eyes lifted to mine, slight panic replacing the fatherly love from before. "What did I just do?"

I chuckled. "I'm wondering the same thing."

A stubborn glint shone in his eyes. "Did you see his face? He thought Santa didn't come 'cause he's bad. Not my kid, T. No way in hell."

Making a low sound, I leaned over, grasping his chin with my hand. The stubble lining his face was soft and slightly scratchy. "I love your fierceness about our kids."

"That boy deserves the best Christmas we can give him."

"We'll make sure he gets it." I vowed. Leaning in, I gave him what was meant to be a swift, hard kiss, but the second our lips met, I changed my mind.

The inside of his mouth was warm, which created a direct contrast to the world around us. As I sank closer, my tongue swept in, reveling in the warm welcome he provided. His scruff scratched against my chin, and I moaned, my hand curling around the back of his neck to pull him deeper.

Cold wind swirled around us, warmth between us. In the background, dogs barked and kids yelled. The scent of pancakes wafted lazily through the half-open front door.

Beneath the gray sweats I was wearing, my cock stirred. I lazily thought of grabbing his hand and running across the property, pushing him into our house, and taking him right there just because I could.

He made a sound, almost like an agreement to my thoughts, and my fingertips pressed a little deeper into the back of his neck.

The sound of a throat clearing above us made me pause.

When it didn't continue, I did, sinking back into his mouth, stroking over him with my tongue.

"Yo, horn-dogs."

We pulled apart instantly, Drew ducking into my shoulder when I looked up at Braeden and Romeo, who were two giants leering over us.

"Enjoy the show?" I quipped, swiping my thumb over my still-damp lip.

"Wasn't half bad." B allowed.

Romeo smacked him in the stomach and arched a brow. "You want to tell me why my nephew, who five minutes ago said Santa wasn't real, now has all our kids planning out some super plot to catch him and his reindeer?"

"And what the fuck is reindeer food?" Braeden wondered.

Drew groaned.

I laughed.

"Family meeting," I declared.

Romeo folded his arms over his chest. "Calling family meetings is my thing."

I held up my hands in surrender. "Maybe you should call a family meeting."

Romeo grunted, and the second he stepped through the front door, he did just that. "Family meeting!"

TWO

DREW

"WE HAVE A SITUATION," I TOLD EVERYONE THE SECOND we were gathered at the table. The mess from our weekly family breakfast was still everywhere. The kids' plates were all sticky and abandoned because they'd rushed off to do exactly as Romeo informed: form a plan to catch Santa and his reindeer.

London and Andi were both in highchairs, making messes with the food still in front of them. I would probably have syrup-covered Cheerios stuck to me for a week.

"What kind of situation?" Rimmel asked, getting up from her seat so she could climb into Romeo's waiting lap.

Trent made an amused sound. "Drew told Travis he was going to see Santa and his reindeer."

All eyes turned to me, and I grimaced. Itching the back of my head, I sighed. "I had to do something. T was out there turning it into some life lesson."

Braeden cackled, but all I could pay attention to was the way Trent bristled.

Fuck. I was just mucking it all up this morning.

"I need more coffee," I muttered midsentence, casually shifting my glance to my husband, who didn't at all appear to be bothered by what I said. In fact, he looked like a giant teddy bear, leaning close to Andi's highchair and happily eating the Cheerios stuck to her fingers. I knew, though, even if it was invisible to the eye, Trent was upset.

He licked a piece of cereal off her thumb, making Andi giggle and my heart turn over.

Such a large man with so much quiet strength. It never ceased to affect me, seeing him with her, seeing the softness not many knew he embodied every time he so much as looked at our daughter.

Andi laughed again and grabbed Trent's face. His nose wrinkled because her hands were covered with food.

Thank God. The thought was instant. *Thank God we found her before Christmas was tainted in her mind too.*

"Drew..." Ivy reminded me I'd been trying to explain myself.

Sighing heavily, I dropped my hand to my lap. "He was crying. I hate it when he cries."

"You can't make promises that are impossible to keep!" Ivy reprimanded, but her tone was half-hearted.

"He's never had a tree or a present. His birth mother told him Christmas was fake," Trent said quietly. "He thinks Santa never visited him because he's bad."

Rimmel made a strangled sound. "That poor baby." Her mug hit the tabletop, and her small body rotated toward Romeo. "This is unacceptable."

Romeo's blue eyes warmed, and indulgence filled his features when he gazed at her. "That's why we're having a meeting, smalls. We're gonna fix this."

"It's our responsibility," Trent declared. "Me and Drew. He's our son. So this falls on us."

"You know we don't work that way in this family," Romeo said, his voice mild.

Rimmel nodded. "We will all do everything we can to make sure this Christmas is memorable and happy for Travis."

"We need a plan!" Ivy proclaimed, her ponytail bouncing with her movements.

"Baby, what plan?" Braeden refuted, sprawling back in his chair like it was too small for his football-player frame. "We already do Christmas like the freaking Hallmark Channel around here. We'll just make sure Trav does it all with us." He spread his hands like he'd presented us with some kind of perfection. "Bam. Problem solved."

Rimmel gasped and shot up on Romeo's lap. "Remember that year we had a horse-drawn carriage come out for a ride around the property?"

Ivy straightened and she, too, gasped. "I know! We can hire a company to come out and totally transform the property, starting down at the gate, with lights and music and take the kids on a carriage ride over the property."

"With blankets." Rimmel was nodding. "And hot chocolate."

"Let's have an ugly sweater party!" Ivy declared. "The entire family can come, and we can do one of those present games." She started snapping like she couldn't remember the name.

"Like a secret Santa," I murmured, thinking back to when I used to work in an office all day and our boss made us do that shit.

No one wanted to do it. Then one year, someone

brought in a candy-stripe dildo, and the boss' wife ended up getting it.

He never made us play that game again.

Braeden groaned. "Weren't you listening? I said we already do enough."

"I'll make cookies with him!" Rimmel plowed on.

"We'll watch Christmas movies," Ivy echoed.

"Decorate everything."

"More than we already do?" B groaned.

"Grinch," Ivy hissed in his direction.

Rimmel twisted in Rome's lap. "Can you get the horse-drawn sleigh out here again this year?"

"I wasn't the one who arranged that, baby," Romeo said, sliding a glance across the table. "It was B."

Both girls turned their big eyes on B.

"Who's the Grinch now?" He smirked.

"Braeden," Ivy practically purred.

I felt my lip curl. "I'm sitting right here. Don't start with that cute pouty thing you do for him."

"If I have to watch you make out on the front porch, then you can watch me flirt with your sister," Braeden cracked, then turned his full attention to Ivy, a wolfish glint in his eyes. "What's in it for me, blondie?"

If they weren't married and if I didn't know he made my sister happy as ketchup on fries, I'd kick his ass.

"Dadadadadada." Andi went off, banging her chubby little hands on the sticky tray in front of her.

Both Trent and I looked.

"You're a mess, peanut," T told her, affection filling his tone. "I'll get a rag to clean you up. Then you can play."

"Down!" London hollered to him when he stood, her arms rising in his direction.

"You too, Lolo," he said, heading off in the direction of the kitchen.

"I'll help," Rim called after him, but I stood up before she could.

"I got it." Waving her back down, I moved forward. "If I have to watch that for another second"—I winced, pointing at B and Ivy being all gross—"all the pancakes I ate are going to make a reappearance."

In the kitchen, Trent was at the sink, wetting some towels. Stepping right up behind him, I slid my arms around his waist so I could press against his back and rest my chin on his shoulder.

"I'm sorry," I said into his ear.

His hands paused beneath the water. I felt a sidelong glance out of the corner of his eye.

"Why you sorry, frat boy?"

"What I said…" I began, patting my palm against his chest. "It wasn't too nice."

The sink shut off, his large body turned in my arms, and then we were standing there eye to eye. We stared into each other for long moments before the corner of his mouth lifted. "I'm not mad at you, baby."

My stomach bottomed out. It always did when he called me that. It was hard not to get distracted by his nearness, by the way his eyes focused solely on me and how he managed to make me feel like we were completely alone when there was a table full of people just feet away.

Still clinging to his stare, I said, "Maybe not, but you are upset."

One shoulder rolled upward before settling in line with the other. "You were right to bring it back down to a more kid-friendly level."

"But…" I cajoled.

He shifted, leaning more firmly against the counter, widening his legs to make room for my body. Without thinking, I filled the space he created, tucking one arm around his waist and fisting my fingers into the back of his T-shirt.

"I don't want him to be ashamed." He confided.

I don't know why his words surprised me, but they did. Even I sometimes forgot just how deeply T internalized things, just how well he was able to reach down into the heart of a problem and comprehend it in ways no one else around me could.

"Ashamed?"

His nod was brief. "Of where he came from. Of his mother. I don't want him to somehow think he's... somehow less deserving of anything because his mother was..." His voice fell away, and I understood he didn't feel like searching for a polite way of saying our son's birth mother was a disaster.

Making a soft sound, I wrapped my arms around him and hunched in, my cheek pillowing on his shoulder. It was okay he didn't finish the sentence; with me, he didn't have to. He didn't have to be polite or even diplomatic, because no matter how he felt, I would accept it. Accept him.

"I don't want him to think he's being punished for shit that's not even his fault."

Like the way my father once made you believe my almost dying was your fault.

"T," I whispered, hugging him even tighter, wanting to wrap my entire body around him like a human shield.

With a deep sigh, he wound his arms around me, and the physical closeness I craved was met. It made me feel a little guilty, as if I was taking the comfort and not giving it.

"This is my favorite place to be."

"In the kitchen?" I wondered.

His chuckle was warm and made me tingle. Dropping his chin, he brushed his lips against my ear. "Inside your hug."

Ah, well, I guess I didn't have to feel guilty after all.

"We're going to make sure he's not ashamed. And we'll make sure he understands what he was born into was not his fault." I vowed.

"I love you."

When I pulled back, my eyes sought his. "I love you too."

The second our lips touched, a goopy sensation met my scruff. Wrinkling my nose, I jerked back. "Andi got more food on your face than she did in her mouth."

"I was hoping your lips would get stuck to mine," Trent mused, wagging his brows suggestively.

Laughing beneath my breath, I snatched one of the damp cloths off the counter and gently cleaned my husband's face. The entire time I worked, he stared, the gold flecks in his gaze sparking like flames.

When his face was de-goopified, I dropped the rag, cupping his cheek. "You're a really good father, T. Better than any father I know, even me. Our kids are damn lucky to have someone like you on their side."

The corners of his eyes crinkled. "We make a good team. Balance each other out. When I get too serious, you add reindeer food."

Groaning, I dropped my forehead to the center of his chest. "What the fuck is reindeer food?"

"Don't you know?" T scoffed. "It signals the reindeer from the sky."

"Har-har." I mock-laughed. He thought he was cute, turning my words around on me.

He was right. He was cute.

"Dadadadaaa." Andi fussed.

"Coming," we both called out at the same time.

When I turned away, T's arm curled around me from behind, his palm nudging until my back was against his chest. My skin tingled when I felt the brief brush of his lips against my temple before he handed me the towel and directed me toward our daughter.

THREE

TRENT

THE HOUSES WERE COVERED IN CHRISTMAS. ACTUALLY, the entire compound was. Ivy called up some company and had them out to turn the entire outside of our property into a winter wonderland.

I didn't even know there were companies that did this kind of stuff.

Frankly, it was overkill.

But all seven kids loved it, so for the next month, that meant we'd be feasting our eyes on colored lights while fake snow clung to our clothes.

Drew was perched at the island, no shirt, low-riding gray sweatpants, and hair sticking up in every direction. Sleep still veiled his eyes, making them glassy.

"Go back to bed." I chuckled, watching him suffer while waiting for the coffee to finish brewing.

"Don't wanna." He grumped.

"Why not?"

"'Cause you aren't there."

Good answer.

Pushing off the counter, I padded my bare feet over

the tile, and my hand delved into the wild strands of his blond hair. He grunted when I pulled his head back so his face was upturned for the kiss I swiftly laid on him.

Languidly, our lips glided together, kissing deep but slow.

A fuss erupted between us, and a tiny cotton-covered foot kicked me.

Breaking apart, we both looked down at Andi, who practically glared at the fact we were interrupting her bottle time.

She was still a little peanut, even though she'd grown so much in the past six months. She was likely going to be small all her life, partly because of the way she was born and partly because it was probably just how she was meant to be.

"Sorry, peanut." I apologized, grabbing the bottom of her bottle and tilting it up. She held it on her own now, but she was spoiled and liked when we held it too.

"Hold your daughter," I commanded, transferring Andi into Drew's lap.

"Where you going?" He practically whined, snagging my hand to tug me back.

Clingy today, was he? The corner of my lips lifted, and I swept my gaze over his sleep- and kiss-rumpled features. I liked it when he was clingy, something he never really was until after his accident.

"Don't you want your coffee?"

He nodded, but his fingers tightened around mine, a total contrast to the yes he'd just delivered.

Little feet hit the top of the steps, and Fry let out a bark, rushing out of the room toward the little boy who sounded more like an elephant as he raced down the stairs. A moment later, the boy and his dog pranced into the kitchen.

"Is it time to go?" were the first words out of Travis's mouth.

He was already completely dressed in sweatpants and a long-sleeved T-shirt with a Pokémon plastered on the front. He even had socks on. They were inside out, but little dude got an A for effort.

Hell, Drew hadn't even dressed himself yet.

"Go?" I asked, pretending not to know. "Go where?"

"Dad!" Travis whined. "You said it was Christmas tree day!"

Blinking, I continued to play dumb. "I did?"

Travis looked at Drew with exasperation written all over his face. "Dad…"

Drew smiled. "It's tree day."

Travis forgot about me and pushed closer to Drew, right in between us to be exact. "Can I use the saw to cut it down?"

Alarm crossed his face. "No."

"But why not?"

"That's my job."

"Well, what's my job?"

"Ahh…" Drew glanced at me.

"You get to pick it out. That's the most important job," I told him.

"I want one that's this big!" he declared, holding his arms out as wide as they would go.

"So long as we can get it in the door." I indulged, then moved off the get the coffee.

Andi pulled the bottle out of her mouth and grinned at her brother.

"You can help too," he told her, patting her head.

"What do you want for breakfast?" Drew asked.

He made a sound. "I don't want to eat. I want to go!"

I was shocked. Travis always wanted to eat.

"You know I can't function without coffee." Drew warned.

"You're slow, Dad."

I bit back a laugh.

Drew made a sound. "When you're my age, you'll be slow too."

"Lame."

"Hey," I scolded mildly. "Where'd you learn that word?"

"Nova," Travis informed.

Drew grunted. "She probably learned it from Braeden."

"Don't call your father lame." Then I amended. "Don't call anyone lame."

Travis's small hand reached over the island to the giant bowl filled with candy canes.

"That's not breakfast," Drew told him, pushing the bowl out of reach.

"What if I put it in hot chocolate?" He bargained.

Kid was a good negotiator.

I slid a mug of coffee in front of Drew, and he brightened. "Sure, why not?"

"Yay!" Travis sang and ran to the cupboard to get the hot chocolate and a bag of marshmallows.

"I thought you were putting a candy cane in it," I said, watching him.

"I like both."

I shrugged and got him a mug of warmed-up milk, and we drank our coffee while he mixed in the powder and added too many marshmallows.

"Can you open this?" he asked, holding out a candy cane.

"Magic word?"

"Please."

I ripped off the clear plastic, and he slid it into the mug amongst the marshmallows.

Drew shook his head. "Kid's gonna have cavities."

"I brush my teeth!"

"Go watch cartoons while I make you an actual breakfast," I told him, gesturing to the adjoining living room.

The second Travis walked off with his mug, Andi pointed in his direction.

"Your sister wants to watch with you," Drew said, carrying her across the room.

Travis jumped up and pulled two furry beanbag chairs that Aunt Ivy bought them in front of the couch. Drew put Andi down in one, and Travis held the bottle for her.

When Drew came back into the kitchen, I spread my arms, and he walked right into them, snuggling into my chest.

"You want some eggs?" I asked.

He nodded but, just like earlier, tightened his arms around my waist so I couldn't go anywhere.

I wasn't in a hurry, so I settled back and held him for a while, running my fingertips up and down his bare back.

A few minutes later, Travis's head popped up behind the couch, and his dark eyes found us. "Can we go yet?"

I started to laugh, and Drew groaned.

FOUR

DREW

FAT SNOWFLAKES FELL LAZILY FROM THE OVERCAST SKY, and the hint of pine and earth mingled in the air, which was crisp with cold.

Trent and I always cut down a tree like this for Christmas, but this was the first year we were out here before ten a.m. Trav had no chill when it came to chopping down a tree. Kid was as fascinated by this as he was about the reindeer.

Oh no, he hadn't forgotten about the reindeer. Much to my chagrin.

"This way!" His holler carried on the wind, floating around with the snow. The red mittens he wore flashed when he waved us forward like we were slow as turtles.

"I think he's getting into the Christmas spirit." Trent scoffed, flashing a smile.

In his arms, Andi was bundled up like a little pink snowman, a thick hat on her head with a giant pom-pom on top. She even had matching mittens over her tiny hands. Even though she was bundled, her cheeks were pink, and it made me frown.

"Maybe we should have left her with Rim." I worried, stepping closer to them. "It's cold as balls out here."

"Your balls have never been cold when I've touched them," Trent murmured.

My cheeks flushed, and I slid a glance at our daughter. *"Frat boy."*

"I'm just saying." He snickered.

"You doing okay, peanut?" I asked, tugging her hat down a little farther.

She made a sound and pointed toward her brother. Guess she thought we were slow too.

"I found one!" Travis yelled, his voice carrying to us. Up ahead, he danced around with Fry, and I laughed.

Quickening our pace, we hurried to see the tree Travis was exclaiming over.

"First tree as married people," Trent informed me.

"First Christmas as married people."

"As parents too."

"Lots of firsts this year." I agreed. "But how about we skip the part where you pretend the tree falls on you and I have a heart attack?" I cracked, thinking back to last year.

"Still salty about that, Mask?" he asked humorously.

"Salt is for fries," I bickered.

"Here it is!" Travis declared, throwing his arms toward a gigantic tree.

And I mean gigantic. And crooked.

"Ah, wow, son." Trent was the first to speak up as we stared at it dubiously. "That's quite the choice."

"Is that a bird nest?" I asked, stepping closer to the tree, reaching toward the hunk of twigs stuck inside.

Something burst out from inside, nearly plowing into my forehead and taking me out. "Shit!" I exclaimed, stumbling back.

The bird gave a giant *caw* as it took off like it was offended *I'd* disturbed him.

Pressing my hand to my chest, I looked at Travis. "Your tree is infested with vermin."

"What's vermin?"

"Bad stuff," I retorted, still trying to calm my racing heart.

"Birds aren't bad."

"Your tree scared Dad," Trent mused, his gloved hand settling on the back of my neck. "Let's find another one."

"It didn't scare me," I muttered, sidestepping a little closer to T.

"You were totally scared, Dad!" Travis announced and rushed off with Fry to find another tree.

"That tree is ugly as sin," I muttered.

Trent laughed.

"This one?" Travis pointed.

"That won't even fit in the door," Trent called back.

"That one!" He tried again.

"Did you even look at that one?" I made a face. "Half of the one side is missing!"

"Can I hold the saw?" Travis asked, rushing over to tug on my jacket.

"No," Trent and I both said unanimously.

Travis pouted.

"C'mon," I said, offering my hand. The one without the sharp object. "I'll show you how to pick a good tree."

I gave the kid a few tips, and then he raced off again in the completely opposite direction.

"I need some fries," I declared, going after him. Kid needed an escort. Who the hell knew what he'd get himself into next?

"Hey," Trent called, the husky quality in his voice making my stomach drop.

When I turned, my breath caught. Not because a brisk wind suddenly kicked up. Not because a snowflake caught in my eyelash. Not even because he called to me with that sexed-up voice that turned me the hell on.

It was because he was standing in the middle of pine trees with snow swirling around. A black puffer jacket made his shoulders even wider than they already were, and the black knit hat pulled low over his head made his stare appear slightly dangerous.

But that danger he emitted was completely contrasted by the pink bundle in his arms. The pom on her hat ruffled in the wind, and as I stared, she reached up to touch his face.

My throat constricted.

My husband. My daughter. They made the perfect picture standing there framed by winter.

"Drew?" Trent's voice grew concerned when all I did was stand there and stare.

The second he moved forward, I made a stricken sound. "Stay there," I demanded, using my teeth to pull off one glove so I could take a photo of them with my phone.

The second I lowered the phone, Trent came forward, took the glove out of my hand, and held it out so I could shove my fingers back inside.

Once I was done, he grasped the same hand and pulled me in, lowering his mouth to capture mine.

Andi laughed when we kissed, and Trent smiled against my lips. A kiss and a smile all at once… I liked it. I liked it a lot.

Both of us turned our heads toward our little angel and tackled her cheeks with kisses.

She laughed and wiggled, and my heart swelled.

Funny how every year when we did this, I

complained about how cold it always was. I didn't feel cold this year.

Not at all.

"You're gross!" Travis hollered, and Fry barked as if he agreed.

"Did you find a tree yet?" Trent called.

"Come see!"

"This one probably has a family of raccoons in it," I muttered, and Trent laughed.

"Ta-da!" Travis pointed to the tree.

It was perfect.

"Now that's what I call a tree!" I approved. "Good looking out, son!" I held out my fist, and he bumped his against mine.

"Do you like it too, Dad?" Travis asked Trent.

"Of course. It's the best tree ever."

I held up the saw, ready to get to work, but Travis yelled, "Wait!"

Going over, he wrapped his hand around Andi's booted foot. "Do you like it, Andi?"

Trent smiled down at him, everything about him softening. Stepping much closer to the tree, he reached out and grabbed a branch, tugging it closer to our daughter. "What do you think, peanut?"

Andi grabbed the branch and laughed.

"She likes it," I announced. "Everyone, step aside."

I could practically feel the heat from Trent's stare as I worked under the tree, my ass right in his line of sight.

"I know what you're doing," I called out.

Trent just chuckled.

"What?" I heard Travis ask him. "What are you doing?"

"Timber!" I yelled, saving him from having to make

something up, and the sound of the tree falling filled the area around us.

Travis clapped, and of course, Andi copied him.

"Now what?" Travis wanted to know.

"Now we take it home and decorate it," Trent answered.

I frowned. "Maybe I should go get B's truck. Load it in the back and drive it down to the house."

"We carry it every year," Trent said, nose wrinkling.

"You already have an armful."

His smile was quick. "You worrying about me right now, Mask?"

"Maybe," I mumbled.

"I'll help!" Travis offered, going to the center and holding a branch.

"Good man," Trent said, then lifted his end. "It's not that far to the house. I'm good."

Once I had the top firmly in my grasp, we started off toward the house, Fry leading the way. Travis "helped" us about three feet, then gave up, running up beside me.

"Can I carry the saw?"

"No!" we both declared again.

Travis made a sound and ran off with the dog down the hill toward the house.

"Remind me to put this thing up where he can't reach it," I called over my shoulder.

"You doing okay?" Trent asked after a few moments of walking. Even though he was slightly out of breath from carrying our daughter and the tree, he was asking me if I was okay.

"Why wouldn't I be?" I asked, secretly charmed.

"Leg okay?"

I suppressed an eyeroll. "I got the cast off months ago,

T. I'm fine." It was a broken leg, for crying out loud. It wasn't like I was crippled permanently.

"It's cold, the ground is uneven, and this tree is heavy." He ticked the items off as though he had perfectly good reasons for worrying. "I know it bothers you sometimes."

I never complained about my leg. Yet he knew anyway. I'd been cleared by my docs with a clean bill of health since the racing accident that nearly killed me, but sometimes my body ached like it remembered how fucked up I'd been. Sometimes the pain was dull and understated like a ghost haunting a house it was trapped inside.

I wasn't sure if it was mental or if perhaps my body just still honestly recalled the pain. I hadn't asked the doctors, partly because I was afraid to.

"I'm okay, T. Honestly." I promised.

He didn't say anything else, and a short distance later, we approached the top of the small hill Travis had already run down.

The second I was able to stare down, I saw Travis running back up—but he wasn't alone.

"Dad!" he exclaimed. "Look who's here!"

Two men strode behind him, Fry jogging along beside the one with very blond hair. Down near the house, a black Camaro was parked.

"Just in time!" I called, stopping in my tracks and dropping the tree.

"Dad!" Travis called to Trent. "Uncle Arrow and Uncle Hopper are here!"

"Hey-hey!" he called out as he dropped the end of the tree.

"This the tree you cut down, little man?" Hopper asked Travis, pointing to the tree.

Travis nodded. "We're going to decorate it!"

"Thanks for coming," Trent told them, coming to stand beside me.

Andi saw Arrow and held out her arms, not wanting anything to do with T anymore.

Smiling, Arrow reached for her, holding her above his head when she was in his arms. "You got big since the last time I saw you!" he exclaimed, pulling her in to kiss her cheeks.

Andi squealed in delight, so I didn't bother to point out it had only been two weeks since he saw her last.

My kids loved their uncles. All of them. But Arrow especially. Probably because he was like a giant kid. I never really thought A would be the kid type, but after he got some practice in with Lorhaven and Joey's two, he was a natural.

Speaking of… "Where's Joey and Lorhaven?"

"They'll be here later tonight. We left early."

Trent gestured to Hopper. "Give me a hand with this, will you?" he requested, going back over to the tree.

Hopper moved to where I'd been, and I frowned. "I can do it."

"Go hide the saw," Trent instructed, lifting the tree.

I made a face. He didn't want me carrying the tree because of my leg. I started to call him out, but he made a sound, cutting me off.

"Mask." He warned.

I relented. Fine. He didn't want me to carry the tree? Then I wouldn't carry the tree.

Bossy bastard.

I glared at him as they trudged past, carrying the tree. He had the nerve to wink.

I waited until he passed to smile.

FiVE

TRENT

HIS MOAN CUT THROUGH THE QUIET NIGHT, MAKING MY eyes shoot open immediately. Another sound filled our bedroom, and he shifted anxiously beneath the blankets.

Leaning over, I found his face in the dark. His normally peaceful expression was knotted in pain and stress. Not wasting another minute, I slipped out of bed and went quietly around to his side.

Cold winter air nipped at my bare toes and made my nipples harden into pebbles. At the end of the bed, Fry's tail beat against the mattress, and I held a finger up to my lips, telling him to be quiet.

Drew made another sound, this one more gut-wrenching than the last.

Leaning over his body, I brushed the hair away from his forehead. "Drew," I whispered. "Wake up."

"I'm here," he muttered, tossing his head around on the pillow. "There's fire…"

"Drew," I said a little more urgently, this time shaking his shoulder roughly.

He gasped as though I'd managed to wake him up, but his eyes remained closed.

A sick feeling twisted in me like a knife, and memories that were heavy and honestly horrifying tried to pull me under to wherever Drew was.

I wouldn't go back there, though. Drew was going to have to come to me.

With his face still a mask of pain and confusion and his hands fisted tight in the blankets at his waist, I slid my hands under him and lifted.

His body collided into mine, my arms curling around him like a shield while one hand forced his head down to my shoulder.

Against his ear, I spoke. "Wake up. It's just a dream."

His body stiffened, then stilled. Even though I couldn't see, I knew his eyes were open and awareness was battling back the nightmare. I waited him out, waited for him to make sense of the world he was in.

The second his hands clutched my back, clinging to me like a lifeline, I breathed a sigh of relief.

"It's all right now, baby," I murmured quietly, hoping he felt the vibration of my words against his bare skin. "It was just a dream, a place you don't belong."

His broken indrawn breath paired with the way he curled closer into my body made my heart stutter.

"T." How one letter could sound broken, sorrowful, and dependent all at once was something I didn't know.

I didn't care either.

It had been a bad one tonight. Maybe I hadn't woken up fast enough. Maybe he'd been trapped there longer than usual.

Palming the back of his head, I held him tight, fingers playing in the short strands of hair behind his ear. "Just breathe," I instructed. "I got you."

His nails dug into my back, and I welcomed the sting, hoping perhaps it would lessen his.

Drew liked to tell everyone he was perfectly fine after the racing accident. He practically hung the docs' physical clearance on the fridge like some exam with a perfect score.

To me, Drew was like a broken vase. One that had been expertly glued back together. It looked great back on the shelf. It was completely whole. But when you got up close, when you held that fragile vase in your hands, you saw the crack still running through it. The scar.

The vase might be back together. It might look good as new, but it would never really be the same.

A shuddering breath left him, and the tremble in his grip relaxed.

"That's a good boy," I whispered, stroking his hair. "You're okay now. You're safe."

The tip of his nose pressed into my neck. His skin was cold. All of his weight was mine to support, and I wanted to push him back into the bed and wrap my body around his. It was what he needed and probably what he craved.

Usually when this happened, I would murmur words of comfort to him or his lips would find mine, asking for a whole other kind of comfort.

My eyes went to the little man lying dead center in our bed. He was bunking with us because Hopper and Arrow were in his room.

When I drew back, Drew resisted, clinging to me. Taking his hand, I tugged him up, grasping his hips when he swayed under the heavy veil of sleep.

"Wha—" He started to ask, and I put my palm against his mouth.

Travis made a sound and shifted, somehow taking up

even more space than someone his size could. Fry lifted his head and looked at us.

"Stay," I told the dog and tugged Drew along behind me.

Shuffling along, he made a disgruntled sound when I hit the top of the steps. I simply let go of his hand and went first. He followed just like I knew he would.

Downstairs, the house was still and quiet, the only light coming from the Christmas tree that Travis insisted we leave plugged in. The lights were multicolored, and most of the decorations were placed at Travis's height and below. The top had a lit star that hadn't been crooked when we'd gone to bed, but now it was.

Drew shivered, so I pulled a blanket off the back of the couch and draped it around his shoulders. Giving him a light push toward the couch, I went over to the fireplace, flipping the switch to turn it on.

Whoosh. The second it ignited, I turned to go back to Drew and nearly ran right into him.

"Jesus," I swore, pressing a hand to my heart. "Make a sound next time, will ya?"

His gaze was stony, and he said nothing at all.

"Come here." I beckoned, leading him to the sofa.

He practically sat in my lap, burrowing close.

The crackle of the flames in the fireplace was the only sound. Soft, colorful lights made the room glow.

"Drew." I cajoled quietly. "These nightmares, are they about the accident or when you were in the coma?"

"Tonight, it was both."

"Talk to me."

A sound of refusal filled the room.

"You should talk to someone—" I started, but he lifted his head and cut me off.

"I don't want to talk about it, T."

"I'm worried about you."

"Don't."

My body stiffened and moved to sit up, to pull him back. He resisted, wrapping around me tighter, but this time, I couldn't give in. The nightmares seemed more frequent lately, and if he thought I wasn't going to worry, then—

"I talked to my doctor." He informed, cutting off my thoughts.

Halting my movements, I gazed down.

Drew's blond head lifted, and his eyes met mine. His nod was brief. "I called him the other day."

"You did?"

"He said the dreams were normal. It's my subconscious way of working through the trauma. Now that my body is healed, my mind will do the same."

"Why didn't you tell me?"

"That accident has dominated our lives since the day it happened. I'm tired of it, T. I just want Christmas with you and my kids."

I felt myself softening. Hell, it wasn't like I was that pissed off to begin with. I couldn't be mad a Drew. It was the thing I was the worst at.

"If you won't talk to me, then you should talk to someone else. A therapist," I said, trying not to just give in even though I wanted to.

The asshole smiled like I had in fact given in and cuddled back into me. The feel of his scruff rubbing against my chest was very distracting.

"I got the number for one, just in case. But I don't think I need it. And if-slash-when I do want to talk, I'd rather it be with you."

I made a harrumph sound. *I will not be charmed.*

I felt him smile against me.

Brat.

As his messy blond head lifted, wide blue eyes met mine. They glowed kinda like the lights on the tree. I tried hard not to get lost.

"You give me exactly what I need without having to say a word."

Well, shit. Beautiful eyes and words? Failure was imminent. I was totally lost. "What's that?"

"Peace. Comfort. A feeling of being safe."

Stroking the side of his head, I smiled.

"You do all of that without saying anything, T. When I start drowning, you pull me back. When those feelings of being lost and alone come back, it's in your arms I'm found. I know you feel like you aren't doing anything, but your presence alone is everything."

My lips brushed his forehead, and then for good measure, I kissed him there again.

His hand curled around my forearm. "Why do you think I cling so damn much?" he muttered. "I need you."

My lips curved up. "I like it when you cling." I confessed.

He mumbled, "It's embarrassing."

"Why?"

"I'm supposed to be stronger than that."

"Thank you," I said, unexpectedly overcome with emotion and trying hard to swallow it all back.

"For what?"

"For letting me see your weak spots. For letting me fill them in. For trusting me enough with everything you have… For letting me love you."

Hearing the wobbling emotion in my voice, he sat up, the blanket sliding off his shoulders, putting on display his smooth shoulders and chest.

"You're the only one, Trent. The only person on this

planet who makes me stronger by allowing me to be weak."

"You're not weak, baby." I cupped his face. "You are strong. And you're also mine."

We settled into the couch, our bodies entwined like we were one and not two. The sound of the fire, the glow of the lights, and the overall feeling of peace enveloped the house, an aphrodisiac I didn't know until now.

Drew's fingertips played along my waist, shooting tingles of awareness along every nerve throughout my body.

"We need a bigger house," Drew murmured, his fingers continuing their perusal.

I made a sound of agreement. "I was thinking the same thing."

When we built this place, we'd never imagined we'd end up with two kids and family who would often come in to stay from the other side of the state.

Joey and Lorhaven were up at the main house. If they'd stayed here, they'd be on air mattresses on the floor.

Hell, we'd been kicked out of our own bed by a five-year-old and a dog.

"After the holidays, I'll call the builder and we'll draw up some plans to expand the house."

Drew grunted, and I assumed that meant he was on board.

His fingers went back to teasing my bare skin, and my own started venturing across his broad back.

"Hey, T."

"Hm?"

"We're alone right now."

My eyes sprang open.

His fingers crept down to the band of my boxers. "Might not be alone again for a while…"

My brow arched. "Are you suggesting we do it here, in the middle of our living room, while our kids and guests sleep upstairs?"

He smirked.

"Someone's going on Santa's naughty list," I mused.

"But I'll be *real* nice to you." His words were punctuated by his body slowly sliding down mine.

I watched, eyes half closed, heart rate already accelerating.

The heat of his mouth closed around my obviously hard dick, seeping through the fabric of the boxers. Sinking my teeth into my lip, I allowed my eyes to drift all the way shut.

"T." He beckoned, a question in his voice.

Fuck, I loved when he asked for it. I loved when he submitted to whatever I said.

In reply, I lifted my hips, making it so he could pull all I was wearing down my legs. He dragged them all the way until they cleared my feet, and he tossed them on the floor. His hands were warm and wide as they slid up the inside of my legs, making my cock jump in anticipation.

Drew shoved one leg off the couch completely, making room so he could fit between my thighs.

When he paused, my eyes cracked open, and I saw him gazing at me as if he were starved and I was a five-course meal.

I didn't think after that because his lips wrapped around my dick and slid all the way down until my tip hit the back of his throat.

Slapping a hand over my mouth, I muffled the moan building in my throat.

He repeated the action until I started to pant and squirm. I don't know if it was mercy or sweet torture when he let go and moved up my body, latching onto my nipple and sucking until it was damp and hard. The soft hair on his beard dragged upward over my neck, and then his lips were on mine, kissing me deeply while my hips thrust up.

The slightly tangy, salty flavor on his tongue was the desire he made me weep, and I lapped it up, the flavor of him and me together on my tongue making me impatient.

His ass filled my hands, and I rocked him, rubbing his dick along mine, kneading his flesh and pushing him harder against me.

The sound of our lips coming apart filled the room but was instantly masked by our heavy breathing. He rose onto his knees, and I worked his boxers off his hips, filling my fist with this thickness the second it was available.

With him on his knees in front of me, all I had to do was sit up to have him between my lips.

His head fell back, and he let out a moan, a sound loud enough to make me pause, tilt my head, and listen to make sure he hadn't awakened anyone upstairs.

After a moment of waiting, his fingers delved in my hair and tugged, silently telling me he wanted more.

Lavishing attention on his head, sucking it deep while fondling his sack, I smiled to myself when his thighs started to shake.

"Trent," he whispered, gripping my shoulders.

"Tell me what you want," I whispered, my lips brushing his head when I spoke.

"You. Inside me. Now."

In one fluid movement, I pushed the coffee table back

and threw the blanket on the floor. Pushing him down, I came over him, pushing his legs wide.

I got up to retrieve what I needed, but he caught my hand, trying to pull me back. "It's fine."

It wasn't like we hadn't had sex without lube before, but I didn't like to. Not when we had some hidden in the next room. Leaning down, I kissed the hand that held me, then slid from under it and went to get it anyway.

When I came back, Drew looked up at me, hand wrapped around his dick, and my mouth went dry.

"Merry Christmas to me," I whispered, dropping between his legs.

A short while later, my slick fingers were inside him, and I leaned up to penetrate his mouth with my tongue. As we made out, I fingered him, occasionally jacking his dick.

Ripping his mouth away, he panted. "Enough, T. I want you."

Chuckling low, I eased out and coated myself with the same liquid already drenching him. I was surprised when he rolled, showing me his ass and the long, lean line of his torso.

Excitement made my balls tighten close to my body and my belly heavy with desire.

Leaning down, I nipped at his bare ass, sinking my teeth in not enough to hurt him, but enough for him to feel it. He jolted, laughing low. Slipping one arm under him, I lifted his hips.

Both of us hissed in pleasure when I slid into his ready body. My chest met his back as my hips thrust, his body squeezing me in exactly all the right places.

A fine sheen of sweat broke out over my shoulder blades, and I felt Drew's legs shake. Wrapping my hand around his cock, I noticed right away how it throbbed, how close he was to release.

Sliding my hand up to that sweet spot I knew so well, I squeezed tight and sank into his ass even deeper.

His body buckled toward the floor, but I held him up just enough to keep thrusting into him while my hand worked his shaft.

My name fell from his lips. And then he said it again.

With one last push, my hips ground against him, and his whole body went taut as he poured out over my hand and onto the blanket beneath us.

He quivered and shook. Small sounds vibrated the back of his throat. I continued to stroke him even after he started to go soft. The second I stopped holding his weight, his hips fell onto the blanket. His body sprawled out under me as if I'd just totally owned him.

Bracing my weight on my hands, I leaned down to his ear, tugging the lobe into my mouth and sucking. "Can you handle any more?"

"Always," he said, his voice languid.

"Truth." I cautioned because hurting him was something I would never, ever do.

Lifting his head off the floor, he glanced at me over his shoulder. "Truth."

God, he looked so satisfied and happy. All I wanted to do was snuggle him close. Going with the feeling, I wrapped both arms around him, my body lying on top of his, thrusting lazily until tension built up and I could no longer be languid.

Making a sound, Drew wiggled his ass against me, making my back arch with pleasure. Suddenly urgent, one hand griped his hip, the other bracing my weight. I went after the pleasure he taunted me with. I chased the satisfaction already written all over his face.

As I moved, Drew buried his face in the blanket and moaned, the sexy sound my tipping point, pleasure practically ripping me apart.

When I finally came back from the blackout of bliss, I fell beside him on the floor, staring up at the colored lights that still blurred together like a giant rainbow.

Drew slid over, draping himself across my chest and tucking his hand between my side and the floor. "Can we stay like this a little longer?" he whispered.

I didn't answer with words, instead wrapping my arms around him, holding him tight.

Drew

Chaos was everywhere.

There were *nine* kids crowded in the kitchen, and the massive island was covered in cinnamon, sugar, flour, and God knew what else. Cookie dough stuck to just about everything, and the dogs were practically tripping people because they were afraid to get the hell out of the kitchen in case someone dropped something they could gobble up.

"How the hell did we end up with so many kids up in here?" Braeden asked, coming into the kitchen with a horrified look on his face.

"Daddy!" Nova squealed, holding up her arms, all her fingers spread wide because they, too, were covered in gunk. "Come see what I made you!"

The look B was wearing didn't last very long because the minute my niece beckoned him, he was mush. "Let's see what you got, princess."

"I added extra sprinkles," she declared, pointing at the candy cane-shaped dough on the cookie sheet.

"Just the way I like it," he said, leaning around to kiss

her cheeks noisily. "Agh! You're sticky!" He pulled back. Strands of her long dark hair stuck to his cheek, creating a long line between them.

Nova laughed and reached out with her hands, threatening him.

"You wouldn't…" B dared.

She did, smooshing everything on her fingers all over his face.

He made a roaring sound and picked her up, flipping her over his shoulder. "You've done did it now!"

"Daddy!" she squealed. "No!" But I could barely hear her denials because her laughter was too loud.

"Rim!" B declared. "Turn on the faucet. I know a little girl who needs a good washing."

She squealed again and smacked his back. "Mommy!" she wailed. "Mooom!"

Ivy wasn't in the room to help a girl out, though. *Where is Ivy, anyway?*

Jax hopped down off the stool he was on and rammed into Braeden's leg. The little guy was no match for his football player father, but hey, I give the kid props for trying.

"Put Nova down!" he declared, running into B again.

"Whoa," B drawled. "What is this? Are you ganging up on me?"

Jax answered by hammering his father again.

Laughing, Braeden set Nova onto her feet, her cheeks red from laughter. "I surrender. I surrender." He held up his hand. "Can I still have that cookie?"

Nova giggled and nodded.

"I'll eat it now." He started toward it.

"No!" Jax grabbed his leg, but B kept walking, taking his son with him. "Daddy! You can't!"

B paused to glance down. "Why not?"

"It's not baked yet!"

"Tell him, Auntie Rimmel!" Nova begged.

Rimmel, who frankly looked like one of the kids but was actually the ringleader of this cookie-making fiasco, laughed. She had flour in her hair, on her nose, and dusted all over the ratty hoodie of Romeo's that she still lived in.

And there was something smeared on her glasses.

How the woman could even see, I would never know.

"Braeden." Rimmel warned, playing along with the kids. "You're going to get a stomachache!"

"Yeah, when you get the poops, don't cry to us!" Blue announced.

Everyone laughed.

"Blue James Anderson! Where did you learn such a thing?" Rimmel gasped.

"You gave the kid B's middle name. It was bound to have some influence, baby." Romeo put in.

"Don't you encourage him, Roman Anderson." Rimmel scolded, shaking a spatula with cookie dough stuck to it in his direction. As she did, the dough flung off and hit Darcy (her dog) in the head.

Ralph (her other dog) rushed over and ate it.

"This place is a zoo." Lorhaven observed, drinking something out of a mug, standing on the other end of the kitchen.

Joey smiled, their son, Jagger, in her lap with a spoon clutched in his hand. "It's awesome."

"Hey! Those are my sprinkles!" Asher yelled when Sophia reached over and grabbed a container.

"We share," everyone said at once.

On top of the chaos, Christmas music played through the sound system, and out in the living room, there was some Christmas movie playing on the TV.

"All right," Rimmel announced. All the kids and dogs looked at her.

Smallest one in the room, but she still managed to command us all.

"I'm putting these in the oven. Who wants to make snickerdoodles next?"

All the kids started yelling and jumping around. Except for the smallest ones. They watched all the big kids, no doubt taking in all this behavior so they could join in next year.

From Trent's lap, Andi clapped as though she was having the best time. Travis grabbed a plastic cookie cutter that was shaped like a star and carried it over to her. Her chubby fingers slowly wrapped around it, and she smiled at him.

"Don't put it in your mouth," he told her.

She put it in her mouth.

"Hey!" He scolded. "I said you can't!" Reaching up, he pulled it from her grip, and she started to cry.

"Hey now, Trav," Trent said easily.

"She's gonna cut her mouth," Travis declared, putting the cutter aside.

"Well, give her something she can put in her mouth." Trent was always so patient. He was better at that than me.

Glancing around, Travis saw an unused spatula with a striped end, and he held that out to her instead. Andi stopped crying and grabbed it, tears clinging to her cheeks.

"Sisters," Travis said like he was exhausted.

Trent and I shared a look, suppressing our grins.

"Wait 'til she's older, little man," Braeden cracked. "She'll be even more work."

"Just what are you saying, Braeden?" Rimmel said,

totally affronted.

"Ah, well…" He coughed.

"Yeah, B." Hopper jumped in, totally amused. "What are you saying about grown-up sisters?"

Braeden turned on Hopp. "What about the bro code?"

"I thought it was sisters before misters," Rimmel intoned.

"Ahh, sis. You know you're my favorite!" Braeden rushed across the kitchen to pick up Rim and spin her in a circle. "What the hell, girl?" he said, coughing. "Did you take a bath in flour?"

"You try making cookies with nine children!" she said, smacking him in the head with the spatula.

"Rome, get your girl," he said, trying to fend off another whack.

"You're on your own, man." He refuted, holding London in his lap.

Knowing he was defeated, B held up his pinky in front of Rim. "BBFL?"

She rolled her eyes and hooked her pinky around his.

"Should have made him work for it," Hopper heckled from the island.

"You better watch yourself," B told him, giving him a sly glance.

"Help me put these in the ovens," Rimmel instructed, pointing to the cookie sheets.

"Yes, ma'am." B obeyed, grabbing one to bring it to the wall-mounted ovens.

"I'll help too," Arrow offered, stepping around the kids and dogs to grab some of the trays and bring them over to Rim. "So, like, when will these be done?" he asked, his blond head peering into the oven.

I laughed. "Kid's hungry!"

For once, he didn't yell at me for calling him a kid. He just shrugged, sheepish.

The second the cookies were baking in the oven, Rimmel went across the room where two big crockpots were set up, pulling off one of the lids. Steam rose into the air, bringing with it the warm scent of apples, cinnamon, and clove.

"Hot chocolate or cider?" she asked Arrow.

"That's a hard choice," Arrow declared.

Travis bounced over to his side. "Auntie Rimmel likes the cider the most," he whispered loud.

Rimmel tapped Trav on the nose. "You're so right."

"Cider it is." Arrow agreed.

A minute later, Arrow was across the room, being pulled into Hopper's lap, a mug filled with Rim's famous cider and a cinnamon stick sticking out of the top.

Before Arrow could drink it, Hopper plucked it out of his hand and lifted it to his lips.

"Hopp!" Arrow whined.

Hopper swallowed and handed the mug back to him. "Had to make sure it wasn't too hot. Don't want you burning yourself."

"It's on low," Romeo informed, sliding a glance at Rimmel. "Because we've had that problem before."

Rimmel made a face. "You burn your tongue one time…"

"More like three," Trent put in.

Everyone in the room nodded.

"Mommy's clumsy!" Asher announced.

Blue smacked Ash on the arm. "Don't make fun of Mommy!"

"It's true!" Asher retorted.

Out of the corner of my eye, I saw Hopper pat Arrow on the side of his thigh. "It's good, babe. Drink it."

Seeing me spying on them, Trent leaned over to whisper against my ear. "Should I try all your stuff to make sure you don't burn yourself too?"

I gave him a look, and he smirked.

"Braeden," Ivy called from behind, her voice muffled. "Help me."

Braeden rushed across the room to take a huge stack of obnoxiously colored items out of her hands. "What in the world is all this, blondie?"

"I know!" Travis exclaimed. "I know!"

I glanced at T, and he shrugged.

"Tell them, Travis!" Ivy told him.

"Ugly sweaters!"

A collective groan went around the room.

"What now?" Lorhaven said.

Joey's eyes were gleeful. "Oh, this will be good."

"Don't even think about it, Josie."

Arrow snickered. "Jace in an ugly sweater. That's next year's Christmas card. Hell, I'm sending them out for Valentine's Day."

"No way." He insisted.

"You have to!" Josie gasped.

"Nope."

"But, Lorhaven, I made one especially for you," Ivy said, batting her wide blue eyes.

"Save those blues for your husband," he quipped.

"Sophia," Ivy called, her voice syrupy sweet. "Come here, honey."

"Oh, hell no." Lorhaven started.

Too late. Sophia was at Ivy's side, eyes wide as Ivy ruffled through the fabric Braeden was still standing there holding. "Ah-ha!" she declared, pulling one from the center of the stack. "This one is for you," she said, holding up a red long-sleeved sweater with gingerbread men ice skating on the front. The snowflakes were glittery, and the trees were made of tinsel.

Sophia smiled brightly, then held it out to Ivy for help.

Ivy tugged the sweater down over her dark curls (that she got from her mother) and helped the little girl put it on.

"Ta-da!" Ivy exclaimed. "Look how pretty!"

Sophia fingered the tinsel trees and touched the gingerbread man. "Pretty!"

"Show Uncle Drew," Ivy said, gesturing to me.

Sophia turned, sticking out her tummy as if it would help me see. "I thought that sweater was supposed to be ugly," I said, reaching down to tickle her. "You're too pretty!"

Sophia laughed.

"Here, now take this one to your daddy," Ivy said, handing her an obnoxiously green sweater.

Lorhaven glowered, but the second Sophia was at his side, his eyes softened.

"Daddy, look!" she said.

"Let me see you," he said, unfolding his tall frame out of the chair and lifting her in front of him. She kicked her legs as she dangled and pointed at the shirt proudly. "Prettiest little princess I've ever seen," he declared, pulling her in and kissing her head.

"You now," she told him, holding out the green fabric.

"Ah…" He grimaced.

"Jace." Joey admonished. "You would tell your only daughter no at Christmas?"

I could practically hear the string of curse words filling his head. Trent cackled, and Lorhaven slid him a look.

"Daddy?" Sophia asked, tugging on his jacket.

He sighed. "Fine." Setting Sophia down on the island, he shrugged off the leather jacket and pulled the green sweater over his head.

Everyone laughed.

It had a giant T-rex in the center, and the Grinch was riding it.

"This is by far the best thing I've ever seen," Arrow declared.

Lorhaven was so close to telling us all off, but Sophia started clapping. "A dinosaur," she yelled, excited.

Jagger leaned out of Joey's arms reaching for his father. Jace took the boy and sat down with both his kids in his lap.

Sucker.

"Here's yours," Ivy said, handing Arrow a sweater with emojis wearing Santa hats all over it.

Then she proceeded to hand an ugly sweater to every single one of us.

"Ivy…" I groaned.

"Put it on, Drew," she ordered.

"Look!" Travis exclaimed, bouncing between me and Trent. "Look!"

We both looked down. His sweater had a Pikachu in the middle with a 3-D Santa hat.

"Awesome," I said, wondering why all the kids were hella cute and I was standing here with a sweater with the golden girls on the front.

"Old ladies, Ives. Really?" I muttered. The ladies had some kind of holiday pattern behind them.

"It's black," she said as if that made it better.

Trent's had a giant plush reindeer head attached to the front. Andi loved it.

Hopper's was blue with a menorah on the front and "Happy Hanukkah" across the top. Romeo's had Darth

Vader wearing a scarf, Joey's had reindeer, and Ivy's had lights strung around it that actually lit up.

"What in fresh hell is this?" Braeden bellowed.

Everyone turned.

And burst out laughing.

Braeden stood there completely horrified, wearing a furry green sweater wrapped in red tinsel and decorated with hanging multicolored balls. There were also blinking lights strung around it.

"Wait!" Ivy called, rushing over to pull up the hood his came with.

More laughter ensued. The "hood" was shaped like a triangle to finish off the tree Ivy turned him in to. Perched on the top of the triangle was a golden star.

"Hells no, blondie." Braeden glowered.

"Daddy! You look like a tree!" Nova said.

"Complete with balls," Romeo quipped.

Braeden started to flip him off, but Rimmel made a sound, stopping him.

"How could you do me like this, blondie?" B whined.

She leaned over and whispered something in his ear, and he smiled. "Fine. I'll wear it."

I threw up in the back of my mouth. I could only imagine what my baby sister just said to him.

"Is this an ugly sweater party?" Travis asked.

"Sure is." Trent agreed.

"Pizza has been ordered," Ivy declared. "Figured the kitchen was messy enough with all the cookie making."

"Mm, pizza," Arrow said appreciatively.

"Speaking of cookies, who wants snickerdoodles?" Rimmel called.

All the kids started cheering. I felt a tug on my ugly sweater and looked down to see Travis gazing up at me.

I leaned down because I could tell by the look on his face that he wanted me to.

"What's up, son?"

"What's 'nickerdoodle?'"

Ah. Sometimes he got shy when he thought he was the only one who didn't know what was going on. All the other kids were sort of at an "advantage" in that they knew all these traditions. They'd decorated trees and made cookies and snowflakes since they'd been born. All this was new to Travis, and sometimes he got over-whelmed.

Part of me worried maybe our big family Christmas was too much too soon.

"It's a cookie. A really tasty one."

"You like them?"

I nodded, trying not to get choked up by the depth of his dark, bottomless stare. So innocent yet so wise. And he looked cute as fuck standing there in that stupid sweater.

"Aunt Rimmel makes them every year. It's a tradition."

"Like cutting down a tree?"

My throat was tight. I nodded.

A big, familiar body lowered beside mine, Trent's side brushing close. Without even thinking about it, I sank a little closer, surrendering some of my weight. He didn't even have to shift to accept it because Trent was always ready for me.

"What's going on down here?" he asked, voice light.

"Daddy says making cookies is a tradition."

Daddy.

As though he knew, T reached up behind me, his palm settling over the back of my neck to squeeze lightly.

My eyes felt damp. I blinked furiously and glanced away while Trent took over.

"Aunt Rimmel makes the best cookies."

"Do you know how to make cookies too?"

"I'm sure I can figure it out. Wanna help me?"

Travis nodded.

Rimmel appeared. Her sweater was dark blue and had a picture of a dog peeing on a Christmas tree on it. She also had antlers on her head with jingle bells that rang when she walked.

"Travis, do you want to help me roll these cookies into balls?"

His eyes grew wide. "You have to roll them into balls?"

She smiled. "Yes, and then roll the balls in sugar."

"Cookie balls!" he exclaimed.

Trent and I laughed. The laugh felt more like a release of pressure that had built up in my chest. It was happy, but it was also relief.

"Come help us, Trav!" Blue called from across the kitchen.

"Yeah, 'mon, Trav!" Asher echoed.

Rimmel offered her hand to him.

He didn't shrink away, but he reached for Trent instead. "Can my daddy help too?"

"Of course," Rimmel answered, then glanced at Trent. "C'mon, Daddy."

His throat worked as he straightened, and I understood exactly what he felt. Travis held his arms up, surprising us both, but Trent didn't outwardly react, just picked him up and started around the island.

I watched them go, taking in Trent's wide shoulders and strong back. Noting how small Travis's arms wrapped around his neck seemed.

I totally got why my son tended to sway toward T when he was most unsure. The quiet strength my husband had was felt by everyone, and instinctively, Travis knew he was always safe with him.

"Everything okay?" Arrow asked, his voice low.

Ripping my eyes off my husband and son, I glanced at Arrow, who was still in Hopper's lap but now had Andi in his.

They were like a pile of people on a stool.

"Don't be dropping my daughter." I cautioned.

Hopper made a sound. "Like I'd drop either of them."

Arrow was still waiting for a reply to his question.

I nodded. "It's all good."

This was actually the first time we'd had Hopper, Arrow, Joey, and Lorhaven here for the holidays. They were going back home tomorrow because Gamble would never allow them all to be away for Christmas Day, but they were here now. They came because they wanted to be here for Travis. For Andi. For me and Trent.

Over the years, all of us had become one big family, sort of like two worlds colliding into one. It all started with a #nerd who was now making cookies with my son while wearing antlers on her head, a football god who, yeah, would probably always be just that. Then I came speeding into town in my Mustang with no clue just how much this place would ~~change me~~. No. Scratch that. This place didn't change me.

It found me.

Football, frat houses, street racers, and pro drivers collided, and now here we were, dressed in ugly sweaters, eating cookies, and being a family formed by loyalty and love.

This. This right here was what Christmas was about for me and what I wanted to teach my son.

"Drew?" Arrow asked.

I glanced around, smiling because Andi was pulling on his hair and he didn't even bat an eye.

"Thank you," I said, my voice suddenly hoarse.

His dark eyes widened a little, but then understanding shone there. Arrow might be a kid, but he was wise. Just like my son. "I could say the same."

Yeah. I guess he could. Everyone in this room could in one way or another.

I nodded.

He spoke up again. "You're welcome."

Joey cleared her throat, and I glanced up. She was watching us, tears shimmering in her eyes.

"You too," I said quietly.

She nodded and swiped the corner of her eye. Then, because I knew Lorhaven was a nosy bastard, I glanced at him.

"Thank you ain't enough to cover this hideous thing I've got on."

I smiled.

"Daddy!" Travis yelled.

I turned.

"Daddy, why aren't you helping?" he demanded, holding up his fingers, which were covered in dough and sugar.

"I thought your dad was helping you."

"I want you too!"

I glanced back at Arrow, who nodded. "I got her."

I tilted my head. "You two thinking about kids?"

"No," they both said at once.

"Being an uncle is enough for me," Arrow said.

Hopper nodded.

"Wouldn't mind a dog, though," Arrow muttered, glancing at Hopper, who groaned. Clearly, they'd had this conversation before.

Arrow sighed at his husband's grimace and turned back to Andi. Over his shoulder, Hopper winked.

Ah, someone was getting a dog for Christmas.

"Do you dare ignore the summons from your sugar-coated son?" a voice growled in my ear. Without warning, arms grabbed me around the waist and lifted me off my feet.

"Trent." I swore, gripping his forearm as he carried me across the room to where Travis was sitting on the island, waiting.

"I made this one for you." Travis held out a crooked, lumpy ball in the middle of his hand that was coated in red sugar.

"It's red," I noted. Rim's snickerdoodles weren't usually red.

"Because it looks like ketchup!" Travis announced proudly.

Nearby, Rimmel laughed lightly.

I grabbed it and shoved it in my mouth. "Best cookie I ever ate," I said around the mouthful.

"It's not cooked!" Travis yelled.

"He's gonna end up on the pooper!" Braeden announced.

"Braeden James Walker, did you teach that to my son?" Rimmel swore, raising her spatula.

He held up his hands. "Take pity on me, sis. I look like a giant tree that Christmas threw up on."

"I picked that out just for you, Braeden." Ivy gasped, offended.

"I like it," Nova declared.

"Balls is a good look on you, B." Lorhaven cackled. "Nice Ivy let you have them back for the holidays."

"I feel attacked," Braeden declared.

"All right, all right. Give the man a break," Romeo said, carrying London into the kitchen while stepping over one of the dogs as though he did it all the time. That's because he did do it all the time.

"Now that's loyalty." Braeden touched his chest. "I'll never quit you, Rome."

London held her arms out for Rimmel, and Romeo kissed them both on the top of their head. "My girls," he said affectionately.

He didn't even complain when one of Rimmel's antlers poked him in the eye.

"Get to work everyone," she instructed. "Let's get all these cookies finished before the pizza gets here!"

No one argued, not even Lorhaven, and we all got to work.

SEVEN

TRENT

THREE HORSE DRAWN-CARRIAGES WERE PARKED DOWN BY the gate of our compound. Yep. Three.

We have a big family, and having just one would mean we'd be out here for years, waiting on everyone to get a ride.

It was cold. So cold that you could see your breath puff out in big white clouds every time you spoke, but the way the colored lights looked against the dark night sky and the way they reflected through the windows of the SUV and shone in my kids' eyes made me think the cold would be worth it.

"I've never seen a horse before!" Travis exclaimed with face pressed to the window.

"They're big and smelly," Drew said from the driver's seat.

"Like Uncle Braeden," Hopper said from the back of the SUV.

I laughed.

"They're going to pull the carriage, Dad?" Travis asked.

Leaning around the seat, I nodded. "Yep, and we're going to see all the lights Aunt Ivy had hung up."

"I would not want your electric bill," Arrow quipped.

Slowing the SUV, Drew pulled off the paved road and onto a patch of grass near the gate. The cars behind us followed his lead.

You could hear the horses' heavy breathing and the chatter of the men who would be driving the carriages as we all popped open the doors, wintry air swirling in.

"I hear the horses!" Travis exclaimed, leaping out of the SUV like he was some kind of cat.

"Whoa." I cautioned, grabbing the edge of the fur-lined hood on the back of his blue coat. "Hold up there, little man."

"Dad," he whined. "Let me go." As he talked, he kept trying to run off toward the gate.

"Wait for your sister."

"Girls are so slow!" He complained.

"We'll walk over with him." Arrow offered.

Glancing up at him and Hopper, I said, "You sure?"

They both nodded.

"He's never seen a horse before." I reminded them.

"C'mon, Dad, please!"

"All right, go ahead. Listen to your uncles."

"You know the gate code, right?" I asked Hopper.

He nodded and then took off after Arrow and Travis.

"Kids," Drew mused, leaning into the SUV to unstrap Andi from her seat. She was pointing at all the lights and babbling incoherently.

It was hella cute.

Going around to help him, I reached for Andi.

He pulled her closer. "I got her."

"You sure?"

Drew's eyes rolled so hard I thought they might fall

out right there in the frozen grass. "I can carry our daughter, T."

Yeah, yeah. He thought I was ridiculous.

Maybe I was. Ridiculously in love.

Holding up my hands in surrender, I backed up while he closed the car door and pulled Andi's hat down farther over her head. "You think it's too cold for her?" He worried.

I grabbed a blanket out of the car and draped it over her. "There will be more blankets in the carriage."

"You cold, peanut?" Drew asked.

She pointed up at the lights twinkling overhead.

"She's good." I observed fondly.

"Hey." Drew's voice was gruff, drawing my eye. "I think you should keep your arms free for a few."

I frowned, not really catching his drift.

"I got this one, because the other one is gonna want you," he explained, tucking Andi closer in his arms.

"How do you know that?" I puzzled.

He stepped close, our stares colliding. The tip of his nose was already turning pink. "Because you're the one I always want too."

I palmed the top of his head, unable to ruffle his hair because of the beanie he wore.

"Horses!" Jax, Blue, and Asher ran by in a blur of coats and mittens.

Ivy and Rimmel raced after them, while Romeo strolled along carrying London.

Braeden was carrying Sophia, and Lorhaven held Jagger. Joey looked like a ski bunny in tight black leggings, furry boots, and a form-fitting white puffer coat that contrasted her long black hair.

"This is ridiculous," Lorhaven declared stopping beside us.

"Ah, come on there." Drew teased him. "You can slow down for one night."

He made a sound, and I grinned.

"Hey," I said as we all went to the gate and the carriages. "How's Arrow doing since he retired?"

Lorhaven glanced at me. "Did you ask him?"

"I wasn't sure if I should. He seems okay, but I didn't want to start anything during the holidays," I explained.

Lorhaven nodded. "I respect that. He's good." He started, shifting Jagger in his arms. The little boy was bundled up in practically a snow suit with a black beanie pulled over his head. He looked like a tiny Lorhaven. Poor kid. I hoped he got his mother's personality.

"Hopper worried that Arrow would regret it and resent him for it."

I nodded, understanding. But I also understood the stress of being married to a man with a dangerous profession and the relief he probably felt when A announced his retirement.

"But my brother was adamant that he was finished, and once that kid has something in his mind, that's it."

"And he's okay?"

"He's good. Gamble offered him a job doing almost the same thing Hopp does, so he still gets to be around all the stuff he loves."

"As long as he's happy."

"I appreciate that."

I glanced at Lorhaven. It was no secret there was no love lost between us over the years. In fact, we pretty much were at each other's throats when we first met. But over the years, our hate had turned into mutual understanding… and yeah, he was my family. I'd probably be hard pressed to ever admit I liked the guy, but with family, you didn't always have to like someone to love them.

Besides, he was there for me and Drew in our darkest moments. He stood with us, and for that I would always have deep respect for him.

And yeah… maybe I liked him. A little bit.

Smiling, I said, "Merry Christmas, Grinch."

I'd have called him an asshole, but his kid was present.

"Thanks for footing the bill for this light fest for my kids to enjoy."

That meant Merry Christmas to me too.

"T." Drew's quiet yet commanding voice carried back to me, and I straightened instantly, dismissing my heartfelt moment with Lorhaven.

My eyes searched for my husband, landing on him and searching around him for anything that could be wrong.

"What's wrong?" I said, hurrying to his side.

Drew motioned across the path with his chin. I turned.

Travis was standing a few feet away with Hopper. Well, actually, he wasn't standing. He was clinging to Hopper's leg, burying his face.

"I don't think he expected the horses to be this big," Arrow said.

"Travis," I called, heading in his direction.

The second he heard me call, his head perked up and his body rotated toward me. "Daddy!" he called and rushed me.

Catching him easily, I swung him up in my arms, his little face burying in the side of my neck. "Jax said I was a baby because I was scared of those horses,"

"You're scared of the horses?" I asked, rubbing his back.

I felt his nod against me.

Realization dawned. Rotating, I found Drew, who wore a knowing, soft smile as he watched us.

I pointed at Travis. *You knew he'd be scared?*

Drew's eyes followed along with our silent conversation just fine. He nodded. *I knew he'd want you.*

I kinda wanted to jump him right now. Like throw him in the back of the SUV and do things Santa would not approve of.

He winked like he knew that too.

Travis's arms tightened around my neck, bringing me back.

"I want pictures!" Rimmel called out.

Everyone gathered in front of the line of carriages so the drivers could snap some pics. Travis made a sound of refusal when I started toward the group.

"Can we take a pic for your aunt? I won't go by the horses."

He did the photo thing, then continued to cling while Romeo and B's kids climbed into one of the carriages. Rimmel's light laugh floated in the air when Romeo lifted her and put her in with the kids.

On the other side, Lorhaven and Joey were climbing into the other.

"I want Uncle Arrow!" Sophia demanded.

Arrow glanced at me and Drew. "It cool if we ride with them?"

I nodded, and they also climbed inside.

Music started playing through the air. A classic holiday tune that matched all the lights.

"Hey, you need some company?" B asked, his eyes going right to Travis.

"We've got it," I said. "Go be with your kids."

"You sure?" He hesitated. "'Cause you're my family too."

I smiled. Sometimes I was still amazed that I ended up part of such an epic family. "Thanks, bro. But we're good, for reals. Trav is just a little nervous about the horses."

"Ahh," B mused. "I totally get it. They're pretty big. And they shit everywhere."

I tried to suppress a laugh. I failed.

Travis giggled.

Braeden leaned over and patted his back. "You need anything, little man, just yell. I'll be right there."

"What do you say to your uncle?"

Travis lifted his head. "Thanks, Uncle B."

"Anytime, kid." He started away, then came back. "Oh hey." He remembered, pulling a carrot out of his pocket. "If you feed one of these to them, they'll love it. Horses are just like big dogs. And we got enough of them running around here."

I smiled. Braeden, the man who would be forever salty about the many animals Rim dragged home. But as much as he complained, he'd never deny his sister.

Travis took the carrot and looked at me.

"Wanna feed it to them?"

"Do they bite?" he asked, unsure.

"Nah." I scoffed.

Andi started fussing and carrying on in Drew's arms. "Peanut wants the horses," Drew mused and carried her over to the last carriage where two large white horses waited.

Drew held her while she stretched her arm out to one of the big animals. When the horse bumped his nose against her hand, she squealed.

"Wanna give it a try?" I asked.

Travis nodded, so I carried him over and stood by the horses, taking care to keep one of my shoulders angled between him and the animals.

The horse turned his head to look at us out of one large dark eye.

"Hey there, fella," I murmured, reaching up with my free hand to stroke down his nose.

Our carriage driver spoke from the seat he was perched on above. "This one is Peanut Butter." The man pointed to the one closest to us. "And that one there is Jelly."

Travis smiled.

Smelling the carrot Travis held, Peanut Butter swung his head toward us, sniffing loudly. Travis made a sound, ducking his head in my neck.

"He wants the snack you brought him," I whispered. "He can smell it."

"Really?" Travis asked, lifting his head.

Taking the carrot, I snapped it in half. "Watch."

Putting one half in the center of my palm, I held it out to Jelly. The horse lapped it up with its big lips almost instantly and started to chew.

Travis made a face and smiled.

"Let me see your hand," I said, motioning for him to hold it out, palm up.

He did, and the carrot looked big in his palm compared to mine.

"Just hold still and hold it out to him."

Keeping a light hold on his wrist, I held his hand out so Peanut Butter could scoop up the carrot.

Travis laughed when the horse grabbed it. "It tickles!"

"He liked it," I told him, stroking the horse again.

Cautious, Travis reached up and did the same.

"I did it!" he said, looking at me with shining eyes.

"Wanna let him take us for a ride?"

Travis nodded enthusiastically.

By the time Drew, Andi, Travis, and then I were settling in the carriage, the first two were already headed off across the property.

We all sat on one side, all smooshed together like there wasn't enough space. In reality, we had plenty of room, but we wanted to be closer.

Travis and Andi oohed and aahed about the lights, which I had to say were better than some displays I'd toured through before, and my hand found the top of Drew's thigh beneath the blankets covering us.

His hand covered mine, giving it a gentle squeeze.

Leaning very close, I spoke so only he could hear. "I'm coming for you later tonight. You better be ready."

Drew's hand tightened around mine, and he turned his head to speak low into my ear. "I'm always ready for you."

"What do you think, Trav?" I asked, resisting the urge to kiss Drew right then. "Horses are pretty cool, right?"

Our son peered up to where the horses were clip-clopping along the paved road. "I like them," he declared.

"How about you, my little peanut?" I asked Andi, tickling her middle.

She grinned and pointed to the lights overhead, her eyes wide and glowing.

"Trent." Drew beckoned.

When I looked up, he was dangling some mistletoe above his head.

I laughed, not even asking where the hell he'd managed to find it. I didn't care. It was an excuse to kiss him.

Curling my hand around the back of his neck, I

pulled him in, our lips capturing and clinging. We kissed gently, lips never lifting from the other's, and I snuck a little tongue in there to rub against his. We kissed until Travis complained and we had to break apart, but before we did, I took the mistletoe from him and stashed it in my pocket for later.

EiGHT

DREW

OKAY, WHO WAS THE DUMBASS WHO TOLD MY KID THAT he'd be able to catch a reindeer with some magical reindeer food on Christmas Eve?

Oh. Right. It was me.

I'm the dumbass.

I was stressing with a capital S. Do you know how hard it is to find a reindeer? You're damn right I looked. We all did.

I wasn't a liar. I told my kid he was seeing a reindeer, so I had to get one.

I couldn't find one.

I was a liar. I made myself into a liar. On my kid's first Christmas, no less.

"Relax," Trent whispered, coming up behind me, pulling me in. Despite the extreme verbal beatdown I was giving myself, my eyes slipped closed, and I relaxed against him.

One of his wide palms rubbed over my abdomen in a circular motion. Inhaling deeply, I reached one hand behind us so I could push my fingers into the soft strands of hair at the back of his neck.

"He's going to have a good Christmas even if there is no reindeer," Trent whispered.

My scalp tingled with the brush of his breath over my neck. My fingertips pulled him a little closer, and his lips latched onto the side of my neck.

Arching into him, I moaned, loving the way he sucked with the perfect amount of pressure. His hips ground against my ass, and hunger ignited inside me.

Spinning in his arms, I kissed him intently, angling my head to invite him even deeper.

A low sound rumbled up from T's chest, and the next thing I knew, he was picking me up and sitting me on the counter behind us. As he moved between my legs, his hands wound around me, delving into the waistband of my jeans to grab my ass.

From this position, I was higher than him, so I dove in, attacking his mouth and rubbing my scruff over his skin.

An incoherent sound erupted from his lips, and then we were kissing again, his fingers pulling at my shirt.

"Travis will be home any minute." I reminded him.

He kissed harder, making my cock throb.

"Frat boy." I panted.

"Mask," he growled back.

Something inside me rose up to that rumbling command. Ripping my mouth free, I stared down at him, chest heaving.

"Are you denying me right now?"

My eyebrow lifted, and I reached down to open the button of my jeans. "What do you think?"

Trent pulled me off the counter and stripped me of

my jeans, flinging them over his shoulder. "Upstairs. Now."

I went, anticipation making my stomach tight.

The second we were both in the bedroom, he pushed the door closed and pinned me against it. His hands were everywhere, ripping our clothes off and teasing my cock.

Collapsing back against the door, I moaned as he stroked me.

"Which way you wanna do it?" Trent asked, his voice low and generous.

Lowering my head, I stared through heated, half-open eyes. "You know."

He was over me on the bed in seconds, lube appearing from I didn't even know where. "We don't have a lot of time." He cautioned.

I smiled. "I know."

He kissed me deep while being very generous with the slick lube. When both of us were coated, he lifted his head. The need burning in his stare was my aphrodisiac.

"It might—"

I leaned up, stopping him from cautioning me. "It won't."

This wasn't the first time we'd had a "quickie," and it wasn't the first time he'd entered me without fully prepping my body. Sometimes, yeah, there was discomfort, but there was never pain. Not with Trent.

Without hesitation, he thrust in.

I groaned as my body stretched around him and then groaned again when his hand closed around my throbbing cock.

His assault was relentless. My ass and my cock both quivered from his expert attention. All I could do was grab his shoulders and hold on as my body rocked with pleasure.

All at once, the orgasm rose up, catching me off guard and making my eyes go wide.

"It's all right, baby," he murmured, the softness in his voice an oxymoron against the hardness and strength in the rest of him. "I got you."

He kept up the assault, and my name fell from his lips as my body arched off the mattress. Curling an arm under me, he held me tight while milking every last drop of desire out of my body. When I was completely boneless, his arm supporting all my weight, he laid me back against the mattress and braced himself above me.

The gentle graze of his lips against my forehead made me smile, but it gave way to another moan when he rocked deep. My legs were shaking when he shouted my name, and his body tightened over mine.

A few minutes later, he rolled to the side and nuzzled into my neck. "You okay?"

"Mmm." I agreed. "I think marriage turned you into some kind of beast."

His head rose off the bed. "Did I hurt you?"

I grinned. "If I say yes, will you stop?"

He pushed up, seriousness replacing the languid satisfaction he had before. "You're damn right I will," he said, reaching for my thigh to pull my legs apart.

Asshole is going to inspect me? I laughed.

"*Drew.*"

"I was kidding, frat boy."

"Your legs are still shaking."

"Guess that means you're good at what you do."

"*Drew...*"

Pushing up onto my elbows, I met his eyes. "Stop worrying." My voice was soft. "You felt amazing."

Some of the worry left his eyes, but not all, so I pushed up and kissed him. "I love you."

That's all it took to soften him the rest of the way. "I love you too."

He bound out of bed, grabbed me by the ankle, and dragged me over so he could pick me up.

"What the fuck are you doing?"

"You need a shower."

"I can manage."

"No, you can't. Your legs are still shaking."

"Don't be so proud of yourself," I muttered. We'd done this a lot of times. I knew his body as well as my own, but damn, dude still got shy sometimes.

We were under the spray when he put me down, locked an arm around my waist, and grabbed the shampoo. "I need help too."

"Can't do anything without me," I muttered, taking the bottle.

"No, I can't," he said sincerely, his eyes on fire even though he was standing beneath the spray.

Butterflies bounced around beneath my ribcage, making me sigh.

I washed him. Then he washed me. Both of us got *very* clean.

NINE

TRENT

"ONE CUP OF OATS," DREW ANNOUNCED TO THE SEVEN little faces gathered around our small island.

Travis, Blue, Jax, Nova, Asher, London, and Andi began scooping out cups full with oats and adding them to their own little bowls.

I should correct. Andi was not really helping. She was just drooling on everything. Travis was making her share. And London was getting a lot of help from her mother.

"Now what?" Travis said, totally excited that they were finally making the infamous reindeer food.

Drew found the recipe on Pinterest.

Dude was totally the wife now 'cause he had a Pinterest account.

"Half a cup of glitter," Drew instructed.

Ivy handed out smaller cups for the kids to add in glitter to the oats. It got everywhere, even in Drew's scruff.

"Half a cup of sprinkles." Drew went on.

"That's my daddy's favorite!" Nova said, grabbing a

big container of red and green sprinkles and dumping it in her bowl. "I'll add extra."

"That's my girl," B said proudly.

Travis grabbed another bottle of the sprinkles and measured it out exactly. "Like this?" he asked, glancing at me.

I nodded.

"Is that everything, Uncle Drew?" Blue asked.

"Can't forget the secret ingredient," he mused, smiling as though he did indeed have a secret.

All the kids sat up a little straighter.

"What is it?" Travis called.

Drew went to the cabinet, reached in, and pulled out a clear jar he'd filled with powdered sugar. "Flying powder!"

"'Lying 'owder!" Asher exclaimed.

Laughing, Rimmel stroked his blond head.

"What's that for?" Nova asked.

"It's to help the reindeer fly! Right, Dad?" Travis said, his voice sincere.

"Right. They need a little help on such a long night." Drew agreed.

He was very convincing.

Romeo reached over and grabbed the jar from Drew. "So if I eat it… does that mean I'll fly too?"

All the kids laughed, and then all tried to get the jar because, obviously, they also wanted to fly.

"Nope," Drew hollered over the ruckus. "It only works on reindeer. Santa's reindeer to be exact."

Travis harrumphed, giving his father a skeptical look.

"It's true," he said, then stole a nervous glance at me.

I winked. It was insanely adorable how committed Drew was to giving our kids a memorable first Christmas.

"Travis, you add it to your bowl first." Drew went on, oblivious to the way I sat and admired him.

The jar went around the room until it was empty, and the white powdery stuff covered just as much as the glitter.

"Now mix it up," Rimmel told the kids, and more messes were made.

"Now what?" Travis asked.

"Now, when it gets dark, we sprinkle it outside on that fresh snow we just got and see if it attracts a reindeer!"

"And Santa!" Nova cheered.

"Him too." Drew agreed.

Travis seemed a little skeptical, but he went along with it anyway. We'd explained to him that if he didn't believe in Santa, it was okay, but he needed to play along so the younger kids could.

"Who wants to watch *Frosty the Snowman?*" Rimmel asked.

Once they were all settled with cookies and the movie, the grown-ups stood around the island, staring at the aftermath of reindeer food.

"Nice recipe, Drew," Braeden teased.

"F you," he muttered.

Romeo leaned over the island, keeping his voice very low. "Gate's gonna be unlocked for a while tonight."

Everyone looked surprised, except for Braeden.

"Maybe have him on the couch around ten?" Romeo continued.

Drew straightened, then leaned into Romeo so close their noses almost bumped. "You found one?"

He smirked. "What kind of uncle would I be if I didn't?"

"How?" Drew asked.

Romeo smirked again. "I have my ways."

"Yeah, a famous face, a famous name, and a fat bank account," B cracked.

Romeo shrugged, unbothered by the truth.

Rimmel squeezed between Romeo and B to wrap her arms around her husband's waist. "I want to see!"

He chuckled and glanced down at her. "I know, baby. I made time for that too."

"What can I do to help?" I asked.

Romeo just shook his head. "Nothing. It's taken care of. Just have him on the couch at ten, and enjoy your son's first Christmas."

My throat closed up, and I glanced at Drew.

"We should help," he said, speaking up for me because I couldn't.

"Consider it my gift to you guys this year, cool?"

I nodded, swallowing down the emotion. "Thank you, guys. All of you. We appreciate everything you've done for us and the kids in the last year. I seriously—" My voice broke.

"We wouldn't have been able to get through it all without you." Drew finished smoothly.

"Stop thanking us," Rimmel said. "That's what family's for. Besides, it was for all of us. I think this is our best Christmas yet."

Ivy nodded and hugged Drew.

"If you really want to thank me…" Braeden quipped. Ivy buried her face in Drew's chest and groaned. "You can let me have the turkey leg tomorrow at Christmas dinner."

"My mom is cooking dinner." Romeo reminded him.

"Ah, it's in the bag, then." Braeden brightened. "Moms loves me."

Rimmel giggled.

"Hand me one of those cookies," Braeden said to no one in particular.

Rimmel was the one who got him one, adding extra sprinkles too.

"You're my favorite sister ever," B said, then grimaced. "No offense, Drew."

Drew gave him the finger.

Much later, the house was quiet, the holiday lights glowed on the tree, and a fire crackled in the hearth. Everyone had gone back to the main house, and Andi was fast asleep in her crib. *Rudolph the Red-nosed Reindeer* played on the TV, the volume so low you had to strain to hear. Travis was dozing between me and Drew, a half-eaten candy cane gripped in his hand.

The presents were wrapped, waiting to be put under the tree, and the grown-up eggnog I'd just had left me with a warmth in my middle.

Or maybe it was just this house. This man. These kids.

My family.

"Hey," I said, glancing down to make sure my soft voice didn't wake Travis.

Drew's head rolled toward me, a small smile playing on his lips. "Hey yourself."

"Thank you."

A wrinkle formed between his eyes, and a lock of blond hair fell against his brow.

"For making my kids believe in Christmas just like you did for me."

Turning a little more in my direction, he slid one of his arms around Travis and pulled him closer. "What do you mean?"

"I mean now I know what it's like to love someone who didn't really believe. All the effort you put in.

Always making sure I had a tree even when we argued the entire time we cut it down. For the lights, the presents, the reindeer food."

Drew laughed.

"But most of all," I said, making his smile fade and those baby blues refocus on me, "thank you for teaching me what Christmas is really about. Love. Family. Being together and never giving up on each other."

Drew swallowed thickly and cupped the side of my face. "There is literally nowhere I'd rather be than here with you."

Even though I didn't like to, I thought back to those days when it was uncertain if he would survive, if our love would die young or if we would survive. I thought about everything he went through, the middle finger he gave to death just so we could be sitting here like this now.

"I know," I answered simply.

"I love you, Trent, and I'm going to love you always."

Leaning over our son, I kissed him softly, then pressed my forehead to his. "I'm going to love you longer."

"So cocky," he grumbled.

I kissed him again.

In the distance, the sound of faint jingle bells echoed. I tilted my head to listen but didn't break the kiss.

The bells got a little louder, and then there was a loud *thump* on the roof.

Travis jolted awake, forcing our heads apart. "It's Santa!" he yelled.

"I didn't hear anything," Drew said. "Did you, T?"

I shook my head.

The bells rang again. Travis leapt up to stand on the sofa, eyes wide. "Listen!"

Another thump and then a jolly, *"Ho, ho, ho!"*

Travis dove into my lap, his arms circling around my neck. "Daddy."

"I think your reindeer food worked!" I said.

"What if it's not Santa?" he asked, peeking up at me.

Leaning in, Drew rubbed his back. "No one else can get on the property but Santa. Remember the gates we have?"

Travis brightened. "Oh yeah!" He patted my shoulders. "Let's go!"

"Go where?" I asked.

"Outside! We gotta catch him!"

"Uuhhh…" Drew stuttered.

"Look!" I gasped, jumping up from the couch with Travis still in my arms.

A pair of legs dressed in red trousers with white fur trim and a pair of shiny black boots appeared in the window.

More jingle bells rang. *"Ho, ho, ho!"*

"Santa!" Travis yelled. "That's Santa! He looks just like that on TV!"

"That's Santa all right." Drew agreed.

"Santa!" Travis yelled.

Kid had a set of lungs on him.

Santa's legs scurried, and then he disappeared from the window and back onto the roof.

"I think we scared him," I announced, making a gesture that we should quiet down. "Santa likes to work in secret. We shouldn't let him know we saw him."

Travis's eyes were wide, and he nodded. "What about the reindeer?" he asked.

Drew and I shared a look, and then we went to the window, wondering, *hoping*, if Romeo had indeed pulled it off.

All three of us looked out the window and into the snow-dusted yard that glowed with the lights that trimmed the house.

A large light-colored reindeer stood a short distance away with large antlers reaching toward the midnight sky.

Travis lost his chill.

I couldn't even blame the kid.

Wiggling out of my arms, he jumped and bounced around and got a million fingerprints all over the window as he exclaimed, "It worked! It worked!"

Then he leapt at Drew. "Dad! You were right! We can catch a reindeer with reindeer food!"

Drew smiled, ruffling his hair. "You like it?"

Travis wiggled down. "This is the best ever!" And then the kid flung open the front door and ran out into the snow.

Both of called his name and went racing after him. "You're going to scare it," I yelled.

"It might be dangerous." Drew feared.

Halfway to the reindeer, who stood there chewing something I couldn't see, Travis stopped and looked back. "No way, Dad!" he told Drew. "Santa's reindeer would never hurt anyone."

Drew groaned beneath his breath.

"Wait for us," I instructed, walking slowly toward Trav, who thankfully did as he was told. Once I made it to his side, I picked him up so his sock-covered feet didn't freeze. "It's too cold for this."

"Please, Dad?"

Yeah, I couldn't refuse him.

The three of us went cautiously toward the reindeer, who just stood there and watched us like we weren't even worth the bother.

I had no idea where Romeo found this thing, but damn, good on him.

The closer we got, the more cautious I became. Drew stepped forward, putting himself between us and the animal. At first, I wanted to shove him behind me, but then I relented. He was protecting his son, and I would never stop him from doing that.

Drew held out his hand, and the animal stepped closer, allowing Drew to stroke its nose.

Travis held his hand out, so I came forward and he did the same.

"He's soft," Travis said, awe in his voice. "What's those things on his head?"

"His antlers," I replied.

"Where's the rest of the reindeer?" Travis asked.

Panic stole over Drew's face, and I wanted to laugh.

"Could be on the roof. Or up at Romeo's house, eating their reindeer food."

"Santa!" Travis gasped, craning his head to look up to the roof. "Look!" he yelled, forgetting not to scare the reindeer. "Santa!"

His little hand pointed up to the roof, and I felt myself smile.

Drew laughed under his breath and shook his head.

Standing partly behind one of the dormers on the roof was "Santa," a huge red hat covering his head as he peeked around.

"Hi, Santa! Hi!" Travis yelled.

Santa lifted his white-gloved hand and waved. "*Ho, ho, ho!*"

"He really is real!" Travis exclaimed, looking between me and Drew.

The wonder and awe in my boys' eyes was something that hit me dead center in my heart. His entire body shimmered with excitement, and his smile was incredible.

Lazy snowflakes had begun falling haphazardly from the sky and dotted his midnight hair and clung to his dark eyelashes.

"How about that?" I said, trying to get the words out without turning into mush.

"You were such a good boy this year, Trav," Drew said, cupping the back of his head. "So good that Santa had to personally come see you."

Travis nodded and reached one arm out to loop it around Drew.

"Thank you, Daddies," he said, hugging us both. "Thank you for Christmas."

The hold on my emotions snapped, and a tear tracked over my cheek.

Behind us, the reindeer made a sound, and I turned.

Travis pulled back, noticing the tear on my cheek. When he wiped it away, my heart turned over. "Are you sad?"

I shook my head. "No. I'm really happy."

"'Cause Santa is here?"

I shook my head again. "'Cause you are."

"Say bye to the reindeer, Trav. He has to go be with Santa, and you have to get in bed if you want Santa to put your presents under the tree."

"Bye," he called to the animal. "Glad you like the rein-deer food! See you next year!"

Drew and I glanced at each other. *Next year?* Shit.

Inside, we carried him up to bed and tucked him in. Despite how excited he was, he fell asleep faster than we both expected.

After making sure both kids were tucked in, we crept

downstairs, exchanging a smile. Drew pulled his phone out and hit the screen.

"You get off the roof okay?" he asked after a moment. I heard some muffled cursing on the end of the line and smiled.

Taking the phone from Drew, I pushed it to my ear. "You have my undying gratitude," I told my brother.

"Love you too, bro."

"I'll see you in the morning."

Romeo grunted, and we disconnected the call.

Setting aside the phone, I grabbed Drew's hand and tugged him along until we stood by the warmth of the fireplace.

"Merry Christmas, Drew," I whispered.

"Merry Christmas, Trent."

Once upon a Christmas season,
A big family came together for a special reason.
Through glitter and mischievous schemes,
A little boy's doubt turned to candy cane dreams.
The fight he caused gave way to laughter,
And everyone big and small lived happily ever after.

GS
GEARSHARK
HOLIDAY
STYLE
WITH
#TREW

I'm sitting here with cookie crumbs and sprinkles on my titties... TMI? Oh well, you all seem to like that here at GearShark, and I'm just keeping it real like any good journalist should. Besides, you probably have crumbs all over you too. It is the season for cookies!

Although, are cookies ever out of season?

It's also the season for some holiday fun, and that's exactly what I'm bringing you with this exclusive, brand new interview today! I just got off the phone with two of our most popular celebrities, and they answered all of your burning holiday questions! So if you've ever wondered what Drew Mask's favorite holiday movie is or what Trent Mask thinks makes a good stocking stuffer (and what doesn't), then stick around because I have the answers!

I have to say it's great to hear from them and know they are doing well after the near-fatal car accident Drew was involved in. Since then, those boys have gotten married, adopted two kids, and pretty much taken over the universe! It's only fitting they take over our special holiday issue of GS.

And might I recommend that this is the perfect interview to enjoy while indulging in some holiday treats and maybe even some eggnog. (The boys would probably join you!) I mean, I speak from experience, as I enjoyed some cookies while chatting them up. Hence, the crumbs.

Without further delay, I'm pleased to present Trent and Drew Mask and their holiday style!

Interview Key:
GS: *GearShark* (Emily Metcalf is conducting this interview on behalf of the magazine.)
TM: Trent Mask
DM: Drew Mask

GS: Before we get to the holiday fun, I must first ask. How are you doing, Drew? The last time we spoke, it was after your serious accident during the opening race of the NRR season. Have you healed from your injuries?

DM: All my injuries are completely healed. I have the papers from my doctors proving it.

GS: That's wonderful news. How was your recovery?

DM: Honestly, it wasn't easy, but having Trent and my family by my side really helped.

GS: Are you still planning on returning to racing?

DM: Yes. But I'm not sure if it will be this season or next.

GS: Why not this season for sure?

DM: <makes an uncomfortable sound>

TM: How about we stick to the holidays?

DM: No, it's okay. Truthfully, it's because I'm not sure if my mind will be ready by this spring.

GS: Your mind?

DM: Physically, I'm all clear, but I still have some stuff to work through.

GS: You mean like post-traumatic stress?

TM: I really don't think now is a good time to talk about this.

DM: <whispers> It's okay, frat boy. I'm good. <raises his voice> Yeah, something like post-traumatic stress. But I'm working through it with Trent and my doctors, so there's no reason to worry. I still have every intention of returning. But I want to get my mind right first.

GS: That's very brave of you to admit. That you're struggling.

TM: <voice much more intense than our usual easygoing Trent Mask> Yeah, so let's back off.

DM: Don't mind him. He's overprotective.

GS: I think it's understandable.

DM: I just wanted to let people know that if you're struggling with any kind of stress or anxiety that it's okay. That it's normal. Even around the holidays. Just because it's Christmas doesn't mean people can't struggle. Sometimes people struggle even more during the holidays. I know it's hard to talk about. <pauses>

TM: <very low voice> *I love you, Mask.*

GS: <Pretty sure I wasn't supposed to hear that. Or print it. Merry Christmas!>

DM: But I thought if maybe I put my struggle out there, it might make it easier for someone else to admit theirs.

GS: Thank you for that, Drew.

DM: <makes an agreeable sound>

TM: Moving on…

GS: Yes, let's get to the goods! Favorite holiday movie?

DM: *National Lampoon's Christmas Vacation.* That shit is hilarious.

TM: *Home Alone.*

DM to TM: I don't like that answer. Pick another one.

TM: You can't tell me I can't like a movie because you don't—

DM: Frat boy…

TM: <sighs heavily> All right. *How the Grinch Stole Christmas.* Travis really got a kick out of that one this year.

GS: Drew, would you mind telling me why you don't like *Home Alone*?

DM: I like the movie just fine.

GS: But Trent can't?

DM: <silence>

GS: <Since this is a phone interview, I can't tell you what his facial expression was, but the vibe coming through the phone was… stony.>

TM: I spent a lot of time alone as a kid. I think it just reminds him of that.

GS: You were alone at Christmas?

TM: <pauses> I spent Christmas Day with my granny and my mom.

DM: I don't like it.

TM: Next question.

GS: Favorite Christmas cookie?

TM: My sister Rimmel's snickerdoodles. They're a tradition!

DM: This year, she put red sugar sprinkles on them for me because it's the same color as ketchup.

GS: I don't think ketchup goes with cookies.

DM: No, but it goes with French fries.

GS: Still addicted to those, I see.

TM: I enable him. Clearly, so does our sister.

GS: Favorite holiday tradition?

TM & DM: <answer at the exact same time> Cutting down a Christmas tree.

GS: Hot chocolate or eggnog?

TM: Eggnog.

DM: Eggnog.

GS: What's your New Year's resolution?

DM: I don't make resolutions because I never keep them anyway.

TM: I just want to be a good husband and dad.

DM: You already are.

GS: <These guys could melt snow.>

GS: Best gift you ever received?

TM: I'm assuming you want something material instead of a sappy answer.

GS: Can I have both?

TM: Drew's heart.

GS: <This is why *GearShark* keeps having to interview these guys. They're totally swoon-worthy!> And the material gift?

TM: Ah, I really don't know.

GS: Really? Are you sure?

DM: He's not very materialistic.

GS: Drew, what about you?

DM: A magic 8-ball.

GS: That's very random.

TM: <laughter over the line> Of all the stuff I've given you, you pick that thing?

DM: It was the first thing you gave me.

TM: Not the first thing.

GS: <There is a very poignant silence on the other end of the line.> So what is the first thing you gave him, Trent?

TM: My heart. Long before he even realized.

GS: Drew, are you blushing?

DM: *No.*

TM: Yes, he is.

GS: Colored lights or white lights?

DM: Colored.

TM: Obviously.

GS: When is too early to decorate?

DM: When you have kids, it's never too early.

TM: Whatever makes you happy is what you should do.

GS: People always need ideas for great stocking stuffers. Tell me what you think makes a great stocking stuffer!

TM: Scratch-off tickets.

DM: <offended> You never get me scratch-off tickets.

TM: Because you'd rather have gift cards to get French fries.

DM: <grunts> Well, fries are better than scratch-off tickets.

TM: Not everyone is addicted to fries like you are, Mask.

DM: I guess I'm the only one who likes to get packets of ketchup, then.

GS: You seriously get packets of ketchup in your stocking?

DM: <defensive> I like it!

TM: You have to get the small bottles of ketchup and the dipping containers. Don't get the actual packets. They burst. It's messy.

GS: You have experience with this, I see.

TM: I've been with Drew for five years.

GS: Drew, any ideas besides ketchup?

DM: I'm getting Trent a pair of boxers with my face on them.

GS: <a choking sound erupts over the line>

TM: *What?*

DM: Kinda like a brand. *Property of Drew.*

GS: Do people often see Trent in just his boxers so they would need this, ah, reminder?

TM: No!

DM: <snickers> Maybe I just want to see if he'll wear them.

TM: <mutters something about him being insufferable> You know I will.

GS: You will?

TM: Of course. If he gave them to me.

GS: Well then, Trent, maybe you should get him a pair with your face on them.

TM: I like the way you think, Emily.

GS: Favorite Christmas song?

TM: "Frosty the Snowman."

DM: "Rudolph the Red-nosed Reindeer."

TM: <mutters> You and reindeer.

GS: Frosty the Snowman or Rudolph?

TM: Drew will say Rudolph.

DM: He's right.

GS: I'm sensing some kind of thing with reindeer… Care to share?

DM: Our son wants to catch a reindeer on Christmas Eve.

GS: How are you going to do that?

TM: Reindeer food, of course.

GS: What is in reindeer food?

DM: I have a recipe. I'll send it to you.

GS: You have a recipe for reindeer food?

TM: He found it on Pinterest.

DM: <whispers to Trent> You make me sound like the wife.

TM: <whispers back> I'm not the one who offered to send her a recipe.

GS: <totally listening> Send the recipe. We'll include it in the magazine. I'm sure lots of people will want to catch a reindeer.

GS: Would you rather have your ears turn into elf ears or have a Santa beard forever?

TM: Elf ears. Same for Drew.

DM: <laughs>

GS: Is that your answer, Drew, or is it what Trent wants?

DM: My answer is what Trent wants. He likes scruff, not a full-on Santa beard.

GS: Fruitcake, yes or no?

TM & DM: <unanimously> No.

GS: Real tree or fake?

TM: Real.

DM: Ditto.

GS: Mistletoe, yes or no?

DM: Why is this even a question?

TM: Obviously, yes.

GS: Have you ever kissed under the mistletoe?

DM: Duh.

TM: Repeatedly.

GS: Okay, boys. One last question. Then I will let you go.

TM: Go for it.

GS: What do you want for Christmas this year?

TM: For our kids to have the best Christmas they can.

DM: Yes.

GS: Nothing for yourselves?

TM: More kisses under the mistletoe.

DM: <laughs> Done.

There you have it, ladies and gentlemen, our iconic couple everyone knows as #Trew (you know you're iconic when you have a ship name at GearShark). We hope you enjoyed this rapid but fun holiday-themed interview and your chance to catch up with the most popular men in racing.
This is GS columnist Emily Metcalf, and on behalf of all of us here at GearShark, we hope you have a wonderful holiday season and wish you nothing but prosperity and good vibes in the upcoming year!

RECIPES

CAMBRIA'S GLUTEN- AND DAIRY- FREE PUMPKIN ROLL

This is a personal favorite of mine. It's pretty well known that I am obsessed with pumpkin, and this dessert is so good. Sometimes my son asks for it instead of a birthday cake (lol). This truly is a wonderful holiday (or anytime) treat!

Ingredients:
  Cake:
  2/3 cup canned pumpkin (not pumpkin pie filling)
  3 eggs
  3/4 cup gluten-free all-purpose flour (or regular flour if you are not gluten free)
  1 cup granulated sugar
  1/2 tsp baking powder
  1/2 tsp baking soda
  1 tbsp cinnamon (I like a lot of cinnamon. Feel free to decrease to 1 tsp.)
  1/2 tsp cloves
  1/4 tsp salt
  1 tsp vanilla extract
  Powdered sugar (for dusting on the kitchen towel)

Filling:
    1/2 cup shortening (I use Crisco)
    1 cup marshmallow fluff
    2/3 cup powdered sugar
    1 tsp vanilla extract
    1 tbsp hot water
    1/4 tsp salt

Directions:

Cake:

Preheat oven to 375 degrees. Line a 13x18-inch sheet pan with parchment paper. Beat eggs, sugar, and pumpkin in a bowl with a mixer. Combine all the dry ingredients into a bowl and gradually add to the wet ingredients.

Spread the batter into the sheet pan. It will seem like there isn't enough cake batter to spread to the edges, but there will be.

Bake the cake for 13-15 minutes, depending on your oven. Cake should spring back from your finger when you touch it.

While the cake is still hot, turn it out onto a clean kitchen towel coated with powdered sugar. Peel the parchment paper off and roll the cake up in the towel. (Begin with the narrow end.) Place rolled-up cake on a wire rack to cool.

While the cake is cooling, prepare the filling.

Filling:

In a tablespoon of hot water, dissolve the salt. Combine the powdered sugar, shortening, marshmallow cream, vanilla, and tablespoon of water with the now-dissolved salt into a mixer. Beat until combined.

Assembly:

Carefully unroll the cake. Spread the filling over the entire surface of the roll. Once coated, roll the cake back up. (Don't use the towel this time!) If desired, use extra powdered sugar to dust the top before serving.

Serve and enjoy!

To store:

Wrap in plastic wrap and place in the fridge.

CAMBRIA'S HOT COCOA POKE CAKE

This is the most popular dessert in my house. I don't just make it for the holidays. I make it year round. It's especially perfect if you want something cool (like if it's always hot where you live), but you still want that hot cocoa flavor.
I'm not even joking when I say this cake usually only lasts two days in my house.

Ingredients:
1 box chocolate cake mix (I use gluten free)
2 cups marshmallow cream
2 tbsp water
2 cups heavy whipping cream
3 packets hot cocoa mix
marshmallows for topping
chocolate chips for topping
hard shell ice cream topping or chocolate syrup

Directions:
Make cake according to box directions, baking in a 9x13 glass baking dish.

When cake comes out of the oven, cool for a few minutes, then poke holes in the cake with a wooden spoon (or anything that will make large holes).

Place 2 cups of marshmallow cream into a microwave safe bowl. Add 2 tablespoons of water. Microwave the marshmallow and water for about 20 seconds. Stir it together, and then pour the cream over the top of the cake, making sure the cream fills the holes. Set cake aside.

With a mixer, place 2 cups of heavy cream into a bowl (make sure its large enough to whip the cream). Add in 3 packets of hot cocoa mix. (you can use the kind with or without the mini marshmallows. It doesn't matter.)

Whip the cream and cocoa mix until the cream forms stiff peaks. Spread the whipped cream over the cake, covering the top.

Sprinkle the top with mini marshmallows and chocolate chips and drizzle with the hard shell ice cream topping.

Refrigerate cake, eat, and enjoy!

NOTE: You don't need to use the ice cream topping. I just like the way it hardens, and I think it tastes good, lol. I've also used chocolate syrup, and that's really good too.

RIMMEL'S SNICKERDOODLE HOT CHOCOLATE

This recipe is courtesy of my daughter. Like Rimmel, her favorite cookie is a snickerdoodle, and this cocoa was inspired by that. She makes this hot chocolate for us every year, and we all enjoy it every single time!

Ingredients:

2 tbsp caramel sauce

1 tsp cinnamon

1/4 tsp salt

1 tsp vanilla

3 cups milk (Use any kind you want. Whole milk would taste the richest.)

1 cup white chocolate chips

Toppings:

Whipped cream

Cinnamon sugar

Caramel for drizzling

Directions:

Heat milk in a medium saucepan over medium heat until it begins to steam and bubbles form around the edges. Add chocolate chips, caramel, cinnamon, vanilla, and salt. Stir constantly until melted. Ladle hot chocolate into mugs and garnish with additional toppings such as whipped cream, caramel, and cinnamon sugar.

TRAVIS'S REINDEER FOOD

Close your eyes and make a wish.
Grab a hefty handful of this dish.
Sprinkle on your lawn Christmas Eve night.
Beneath the moon, it will sparkle bright.
Santa's reindeer will be flying high.
This will guide them to you from the sky.

*NOTE: This is **not** edible. If you want it to be edible, do not use glitter or purchase edible glitter.*

Ingredients:

1 cup oats (a reindeer favorite!)
1/2 cup glitter
1/2 holiday sprinkles
1/4 cup flying powder (aka powdered sugar)

Directions:

Mix all ingredients in a bowl. Place in a bag or container.

Sprinkle on your lawn Christmas Eve night!

GINGERBREAD CUPCAKES WITH CINNAMON VANILLA FROSTING

These cupcakes sound mouthwatering and are also a new take on gingerbread if you are used to eating the traditional gingerbread man! Bonus points because these don't have legs to run off!

Ingredients
- 1/2 cup butter (1 stick)
- 1/2 cup dark brown sugar
- 1 egg
- 1/2 cup molasses
- 1/2 cup milk
- 1 1/2 cups flour
- 1 tsp baking soda
- 1 1/2 tsp ground cinnamon
- 1 tsp ground ginger
- 1/2 tsp ground nutmeg
- 1/4 tsp ground allspice
- 1/4 tsp salt

Frosting:

1/2 cup butter (Use room temperature. Cold butter will not mix.)

1 tbsp vanilla extract

1 tsp cinnamon

2 cups powdered sugar

Directions:

Preheat oven to 350 degrees.

Using an electric mixer, beat the butter and dark brown sugar. Then add the molasses and egg. Blend until combined. Gradually add the milk, flour, spices, salt, and baking soda and mix until combined.

Mix the flour, baking soda, ground cinnamon, ground ginger, ground nutmeg, ground allspice, and salt in a medium bowl. Stir well.

Spray your cupcake pan with nonstick spray OR use cupcake liners. Fill 2/3 of the way full with batter.

Bake cupcakes for approximately 18 minutes (depending on your oven) or until a toothpick inserted into the center comes out clean. Let cupcakes cool, then frost with cinnamon vanilla frosting.

Frosting:

Combine all the ingredients in a bowl. Using an electric mixer, beat until fluffy and combined. If the icing is too thick, you can add milk to thin it out. Be sure to add small amounts at a time! If the icing is too thin, you can add a bit more powdered sugar.

NOTE: It is always best to use room temperature ingredients when making cupcakes, so let the egg, milk, and butter (any cold ingredient) set out for a bit before making your cupcakes and frosting.

ALSO NOTE: This recipe is one I found on Pinterest.

GRINCH PANCAKES

Perfect for pancake Sundays... or any day! So tasty they just might make your heart grow three sizes!

Ingredients:
    1 1/4 cups buttermilk
    1/4 cup sugar
    2 tbsp melted butter
    1 tsp vanilla extract
    1 1/4 cups all-purpose flour
    1/8 tsp salt
    1 tsp baking powder
    1 tsp baking soda
    1 egg
    Green food coloring

Whipped cream:
    2 cups heavy whipping cream
    4 tbsp powdered sugar
    2 tsp vanilla extract
    Green food coloring

Directions:

Pancakes:

In a large bowl, mix dry ingredients together. Whisk in melted butter, egg, vanilla, and buttermilk. Whisk until all combined. Batter may still have lumps. Add green food coloring until desired color is achieved.

Use a greased skillet over medium heat and ladle about 1/4 cup of batter into warm pan. When the edges of the pancake are set and bubbles have formed on the surface, flip pancakes and cook until lightly browned. Removed cooked pancakes to a platter.

Whipped cream:

Combine whipping cream, sugar, and vanilla in a large bowl. Add a few drops of green food coloring. Using electric mixer, beat the cream on high speed until it forms stiff peaks.

Serving:

Plate a few pancakes and add a dollop of the grinchy whipped cream onto the top. Garnish with red sprinkles. Butter and syrup are also great additions!

NOTE: I found the recipe for the pancakes online.

CINNAMON ORNAMENTS

*These are perfect for hanging on the tree or using as gift tags
and make a fun craft for you and the family! Many years ago,
I made these with my mom, and we hung them on our tree.
They lasted so long. You can definitely save them from year to
year to reuse them.*
*Please note, these ornaments are NOT edible, but they
wouldn't hurt you if you took a bite!*

What you need:
    3/4 cup ground cinnamon
    1 tbsp ground allspice
    2 tbsp ground cloves
    1 tbsp ground nutmeg
    1 cup applesauce
    Copper wire
    String or ribbon for hanging

Directions:
Combine cinnamon, allspice, cloves, nutmeg, and
applesauce into a bowl and mix thoroughly. Mixture will

be stiff. Roll out dough onto a floured surface to roughly 1/4-inch thickness. Using your favorite cookie cutters (small or medium shapes work well) cut the dough into your favorite holiday shapes. Move ornaments onto a greased cookie sheet.

Repeat with excess dough until it's all used up!

Cut the copper wire into 2-inch pieces. Bend the wire into a horseshoe shape. Insert the wire into the tops of your ornaments, leaving the open end at the top. This step results in creating a hole in the top of your ornament for hanging.

Leave the ornaments uncovered to dry for four to five days. Yes. Days.

To hang or use as a gift tag:

Use precut pieces of ribbon (you choose the color!), push one end under the wire, and loop through. Tie ends together at the top, creating a knot. You can use additional ribbon to make a bow if you desire.

Store the dried ornaments in a plastic container and use from year to year!

SNICKERDOODLES

This recipe was previously seen in #Holiday (The Hashtag Series). *I chose to share this recipe in this book as well because these cookies are a tradition for the entire family. Plus, if you haven't read* The Hashtag Series, *then you will still get Rimmel's favorite cookie recipe!*

Ingredients:
1/2 cup butter (1 stick)
1/2 cup shortening
1 1/2 cups sugar
2 eggs
1 tsp vanilla
2 3/4 cups flour
2 tsp cream of tartar
1 tsp baking soda
1/4 tsp salt
Cinnamon and sugar mixture to roll cookies in

Directions:
Preheat oven to 375 degrees.

Mix together all the wet ingredients, then add in all the dry.

Shape dough into small balls.

Roll each ball in mixture of cinnamon and sugar.

Place each ball 2 inches apart on a cookie sheet.

Bake the cookies at 375 for 8-10 minutes or until just slightly brown.

Remove cookies from oven and transfer to aluminum foil to cool.

RIMMEL'S APPLE CIDER

This recipe was previously seen in the Hashtag Series. *I chose to share this recipe in this book as well because it's mentioned. I know several readers who make this, and they give it two thumbs up!*

Ingredients:
64 ounces apple cider
3 cinnamon sticks
1 tsp allspice
1 tsp whole cloves
1/3 cup brown sugar

Directions:

Combine the cider, cinnamon sticks, and sugar in a slow cooker. Wrap the allspice and cloves in a cheese-cloth and place inside. (The cheesecloth makes it easier to remove the seasonings later.) Bring to a boil, then reduce heat and simmer on low for one hour.

Garnish with apple slices, a cinnamon stick, and whipped cream if desired.

AUTHOR'S NOTE

I hope you read this novella with a smile on your face and warmth in your heart. I know it's hard to say goodbye to such beloved characters, and I know many readers would like me to continue writing about them forever! The *GearShark* characters are in wonderful places right now, and I think this is the perfect place to leave off—with *happily ever after*.

These characters will always be part of my family and in my heart. I can't say that we won't ever see them again. Maybe we will. But this is the end of the *GearShark* series.

Leaving off on this sweet, light note is my holiday gift to you. Even if you don't celebrate the traditional holidays, hopefully you enjoyed the antics of a bunch of men trying to give their kids the most memorable childhood they can.

Also, please know how grateful I am to you for all your support!

May the new year bring you all peace, joy, and success in whatever goals you work toward!

PS: Don't forget to put out the reindeer food!

See you next book!

~XOXO~
Cambria

Cambria Hebert is a bestselling novelist of more than fifty titles. She went to college for a bachelor's degree, couldn't pick a major, and ended up with a degree in cosmetology. So rest assured her characters will always have good hair.

Besides writing, Cambria loves a pumpkin spice latte, staying up late, sleeping in, and watching K drama until her eyes won't stay open. She considers math human torture and has an irrational fear of chickens (yes, chickens). You can often find her running on the treadmill (she'd rather be eating a donut), painting her toenails (because she bites her fingernails), or walking her chihuahuas (the real bosses of the house).

Cambria has written in many genres, including new adult, sports romance, male/male romance, sci-fi, thriller, suspense, contemporary romance, and young adult. Many of her titles have been translated into foreign languages and have been the recipients of multiple awards.

Awards Cambria has received include:

Author of the Year 2016 (UtopiaCon2016)
The Hashtag Series: Best Contemporary Series of 2015
(UtopiaCon 2015)
#Nerd: Best Contemporary Book Cover of 2015
(UtopiaCon 2015)
Romeo from the Hashtag Series: Best Contemporary
Lead (UtopiaCon 2015)
#Nerd: Top 50 Summer Reads (Buzzfeed.com 2015)
The Hashtag Series: Best Contemporary Series of 2016
(UtopiaCon 2016)
#NERD Book Trailer: Best Book Trailer of 2016
(UtopiaCon 2016)
#Nerd Book Trailer: Top 50 Most Cinematic Book
Trailers of All Time (film-14.com)
#Nerd: Book Most Wanted to be Adapted to Screen:
(2018)
Amnesia: Mystery Book of the Year (2018)

Cambria Hebert owns and operates Cambria Hebert
Books, LLC.
You can find out more about Cambria and her titles by
visiting her website:
http://www.cambriahebert.com